Judge Parker's Lawmen

'Are those fellas at the crick going to shoot at us, Marshal?' a confused Zeke asked.

Marshal Houseman gave his deputy a fierce twist of a grin. 'I reckon they will, boy, when we go fire-ballin' in on them doin' some shooting of our own.'

Much to Marshal Housman's displeasure, 'Hanging' Judge Parker has sent him and his greenhorn deputy, Zeke Butler, to put paid to a band of raiders who are burning out Indian farmers in the Cherokee Strip in Indian Territory.

With the aid of Bear Paw, a newly reformed drunk, and some of his kin, the two lawmen face the raiders in a series of shoot-outs which confirms Zeke as one of the Judge's toughest manhunters.

By the same author

The Man From Shiloh
The Last of the Marauders
The Buffalo Soldier
The Owlhooter
The Cattle Lifters
The Maverick
The Dude
The Pinkerton
The Loner
The Greenhorn
The Gringo General
The Peace Officer
The Chickamaugo Covenant
The Compadres
The Last of the Old Guns
The Beholden Man
A Kansas Bloodletting
The Panhandle Shoot-Out
The President's Man
The Law-Bringers
Trouble on the Lordsburg Trail
Woodrow's Last Heist
The Blue-Belly Sergeant
The Return of the Gringo
The Man from Clay County
The San Pedro Ring
Tucumcari Shoot-Out
The Devil's Deacon
The Vengeance Seekers
The Regulators
War on the Pecos
The Missouri Raiders
The Killing of El Lobo
The High Plains Killings
The Making of an Hombre
Horse Thief Trail
The Redemption Trail
The Frontiersmen
The High Country Yankee
The Johnson County Shootings
The Jayhawkers
Hard Men Riding

Judge Parker's Lawmen

Elliot Conway

A Black Horse Western

ROBERT HALE · LONDON

© Elliot Conway 2007
First published in Great Britain 2007

ISBN 978-0-7090-8500-3

Robert Hale Limited
Clerkenwell House
Clerkenwell Green
London EC1R 0HT

www.halebooks.com

Typeset by
Derek Doyle & Associates, Shaw Heath
Printed and bound in Great Britain by
Antony Rowe Limited, Wiltshire

For Susan and Jeff Munro and biscuit days at Sandhill.

ONE

Adam Paxton stepped out of his shack and walked over to the run of high ground that stretched across his land at the rear of the hay barn. He was carrying a rifle and a belted pistol about his middle, thinking that things had come to a sorry pass when come nightfall a man could not walk across his back yard without being armed up as though he was going to war. Which, when he thought about it, was what he was doing, though he didn't know who his enemies were and why the unkown bastards had raided his farm.

He climbed up the steep slope to the ridge and the blanket-wrapped figure of his son, David, standing the first watch. 'Everything OK, Son?' he asked. 'Heard or seen anything?'

'No, Pa,' replied David. 'Nothin' but a coupla wolves sniffin' around.'

'OK, then,' Adam said. 'You go and get that bowl of soup Ma's left out for you then get some sleep in, we've got a busy day tomorrow. I'll stand watch the rest of the night.'

After his son had made his way down the slope Paxton wrapped himself up in the blanket and settled down for four hours of a lonely, cold vigil. One of many he and his boy had stood since the night of the raid on his farm. Paxton's face grimmed over. And the gunning down of old Ben Lawson, his hired hand.

Bessie, his mare, was having a long and difficult labour and he and Ben were sitting up with her. It must have been two o'clock or so when the mare gave signs of giving birth.

'Go and get those pails of water, Ben,' he had said, 'that Liz said she'd keep on the boil.'

Ben had picked up one of the storm lanterns and hurried out of the barn.

Paxton shivered and drew the blanket closer about him. Whether it was the cold wind blowing across the ridge or the vivid remembering of that night that was giving him the chills, he wasn't sure. A bit of both, he opined.

Ben couldn't have made it more than halfway to the house when the riders come thundering in. He heard men calling to each other then a single gunshot.

With a gasped, 'What the hell!' he was up on to his feet, the imminent birth of a foal forgotten. He grabbed hold of the rifle he had taken to the barn with him to scare off any wolves hungry and bold enough to come prowling close to the outbuildings, and dashed out of the barn levering a shell into the firing chamber.

Though there was no moon there was enough light from the stars and the flaming torches several of the riders held for him to see that it was a considerable band of raiders who had descended on his farm. Cursing, he brought up his rifle and cut loose at them as fast as he could draw back the hammer. He had an easy target. He heard men and horses cry out in pain and shouts of alarm from the now swirling mass of riders. Then he had to duck back into the barn as return fire from the raiders tore lumps out of the door-posts and planking.

Paxton dropped his empty rifle and drew out his pistol and, mad-assed angry at the sons-of-bitches who had come to burn him out, stepped out into the open again and fanned off the six loads in one rapid burst of gunfire and was rewarded by hearing more cries of pain and a shouted, 'The bastard's winged me!' though now he was standing up against the raiders with both of his guns emptied. Yet still too angry to feel any fear knowing that if any of the raiders made a rush for him he'd be dead. He darted back into the barn as another hail of lead came his way and began thumbing reloads into the chambers of his Colt.

A rifle and a shotgun firing from the house brought a grim smile on Paxton's face. The odds were begin-ning to swing in his favour. David and Ma were backing him up. Between them they had the raiders boxed in. As if to prove his point he heard a shout of, 'Let's get to hell outa here, boys!'

Then the raiders were gone as quickly as they had shown up. Paxton waited a moment or two till the dust of their going had settled somewhat before he walked warily out into the open.

'Are you're OK, Pa?' Dave called out, as he stepped out on to the porch.

'I'm all right, boy,' Paxton replied. 'Are Ma and Sarah Jane OK?'

'Yeah,' said David. 'It was Sarah Jane who was firin'

the shotgun. Who were they, Pa?'

'Well I'll be durned,' Paxton muttered. 'I've a shootist for a daughter.' Raising his voice he said, 'I don't know who they were but that ain't my worry for the moment, Ben's out here somewhere. Keep your rifle handy when you step down from the porch. We've downed some of the sonsuvbitches but they could be only wounded and still mean enough to do what they came here to do.'

One of the night riders' torches, lying on the ground, was still alight. Paxton bent down and picked it up, whirled it about his head two, three times until the flickering yellow flames flared bright red.

By its light Paxton and his son, fingers taking up the first pressure on the triggers of their guns, toed the dead raiders' bodies, five in all, to make certain that they were no longer a threat to them. They found Ben's body lying in a crumpled heap part way under the porch. Paxton dropped to his knees alongside it. The hand he placed on Ben's chest to feel if the old man was still breathing came away warm and sticky with blood. Cursing softly he got back on to his feet.

'Whoever the sonsuvbitches were, Dave,' he said, hard-voiced, 'they've killed Ben. But at a price they'll have not been willin' to pay.' Then Paxton remembered why he and Ben had been up so late. 'Ma!' he called out to his wife who, along with his daughter, were now standing on the porch. 'Go into the barn and see to Bessie; me and Dave will clear up here.' Paxton noticed that his daughter was still holding the shotgun. 'You did good work, girl,' he said. 'You've got your ma's plainswoman's blood in you.'

Sarah Jane didn't feel as though she was as strong willed as her mother. She had fired the shotgun with her eyes practically closed. She was still shaking. But she gave her pa a wan but confident smile.

Early next morning Paxton drove into Bitter Water Springs with his flat-bed wagon loaded with the bodies of the dead raiders. By the time he pulled up outside the sheriff's office a small crowd had collected to get a closer look, and comment, on the wagon's grisly load. Sheriff Blakemore, hearing all the talking going on, came out of his office to see what all the fuss was about.

He stopped in his tracks as he saw the pile of dead bodies. 'Sweet Jesus!' he gasped, his face paling. 'Have you been partakin' in a small war, Adam? You'd better step inside and tell me all about it.' Before following Adam inside he gave orders to a couple of his deputies to take the wagon along to the mortician's but to check out the bodies first to see if any of them had warrants posted on them.

Sheriff Blakemore came out with another disbelieving, 'Sweet Jesus!' after hearing about the raid and the killing of Ben.

'I've heard tell of other suchlike raids against some Injun farms west of here, Adam,' he said, 'but I put that down to a bunch of gun-happy assholes who don't take kindly to Injuns owning land. You bein' raided is the first against a white-eye's farm. M'be they took your place for an Injun holding? I'll do what I can to find out who the murdering sonsubitches are, but being that I've only got three deputies, Injun boys, whose main job, is to make sure that their kinfolk don't get

11

liquored up and go back to their old heathen ways, liftin' us white-eyes' hair, we ain't big enough to take on a bunch of barn-burnin' night riders.'

'What about Judge Parker?' Adam asked. 'Ain't he supposed to uphold the law here? He's got a whole army of deputy marshals at his callin'.'

'That he has, Adam,' the sheriff replied. 'Hard men, too. But the judge's law doesn't reach into the Cherokee Strip. The Injun Bureau runs things this side of the line. I reckon they'll have already raised posses to track down the raiders. I'll let the county marshal know about your place bein' hit.'

With an angry, 'Don't bother, Sheriff, I'll see to things myself!' Adam got to his feet and stormed out of the office and strode purposefully along the boardwalk to the Western Union telegraph office. To hell with the sheriff telling him who ran the law in the territory, he would ask Judge Isaac Parker if he would despatch some of his 'Hang 'em high' law to the Strip. Adam knew that the judge didn't hold having any restrictions, legal or otherwise, against him carrying out the law as he saw it. The old bastard would send his deputies to Hell to rope in the Devil if the mood took him so.

Wes Stacey, a ploughshare-faced man, stood at the bar of the Long Branch saloon, his drink standing untouched in front of him, and feeling mean-minded enough to pull out his pistol and shoot up the whole bar just to ease his angry frustrated feelings. At one of the nearby tables sat the last of the men who rode with him – three of them. And by their pinched-assed faces they wouldn't be taking any more orders from him.

Not when he had led them blindly into a sodbuster's ambush that had got five of their buddies dead.

He scowled at his reflection in the bar mirror, cursing at how his luck had suddenly and unexpectedly gone all to hell. The shyster lawyer who had hired him to harass the Indian sodbusters had told him that raiding lonely family-run farms would be less dangerous than robbing banks and stages. And the mealy-mouthed bastard had smiled when he said it. Stacey cut loose with a growled string of curses. He couldn't see any smiles on the faces of the three at the table drinking whiskey as though they were going to sign the pledge when they got through the bottle. And there sure wouldn't be any smiles on the boys' faces they had left lying in the dirt in front of that sodbuster's shack. Though to be fair, the big man back East, whom the lawyer was fronting for, was a good payer. It was like getting money from home. And the shyster had been right, they had put the torch to four Indian-run farms without a shot fired at them. Then he'd had more than half of his gang wiped out in a few minutes of gun hell.

His hiring had began a couple of months ago. He had been standing at this very bar when the store-suited dude came alongside him and only looking at him in the bar mirror said, without a 'Howdie', 'My name is Frazer, Mr Stacey, I'm a lawyer representing some important business interests based in Chicago. My employers wish you to do a job of work for them.' Frazer gave a slight nervous cough. 'It is sort of illegal, but you and the men you will need to hire will be well compensated for your trouble.'

Stacey straightened himself up from the bar and

wary-eyed the lawyer back through the mirror, wondering how the dude knew who he was. He saw a smooth cheeked face as unreadable as an Indian buck's. . . .

'What makes you think I'd be willin' to partake in any chore that's agin the law, mister?' he asked.

Stacey saw the ghost of a smile bring a little life into the bland-featured face.

'I know all about your former activities, Mr Stacey,' Frazer replied. 'You have robbed banks, stages and stolen cattle, killed at least four men in doing so. If you put one foot out of the Cherokee Strip, Judge Parker's marshals will grab you and you'll end up at Fort Smith, next in line to swing on the judge's fine gallows.'

Stacey stiffened in anger and his hand crept down to his pistol butt.

'Come, come, Mr Stacey,' Frazer told him. 'There's no need to take umbrage. I'm only relating something that everyone already knows about you. It's the reason why I want to hire you.' Stacey glimpsed Frazer's lip-curling smile again. 'Good hired help is hard to come by, Mr Stacey, and my principal is willing to pay highly to get it.'

Stacey calmed down somewhat. The lawyer was right, even the dogs in the territory knew he had a rep as a badman. Spending money was always a problem with him. Robbing a bank or a stage here in the Strip would be as though he was asking to be put in a cell. He shot a narrow-eyed glance at the lawyer's mirror likeness.

'Tell me about this illegal work your boss back there in Chicago wants doin', lawyer man,' he said

In a few dry sentences the lawyer told Stacey what would be expected of him. Stacey quickly weighed up

14

the risks to his well-being burning out Indian sodbusters. He couldn't come up with any.

He would have to get himself a gang of sorts, which
would be no problem. The Strip was crawling with lawbreaking men struggling to find their wherewithal as
he was. What the big man in Chicago wanted the
Indian land for was no business of his. The dude could
be thinking that there was gold in the soil.

He heard the lawyer say, 'Take a day or so to think
about my proposal, Mr Stacey. I know you will have to
hire suitable men, I'll leave all that to you. Then, when
you come up with a price, I'll see if it is favourable to
my client. But it is not wise for us to meet in here again.
When you have got the men you need, meet me at that
abandoned shack on the east trail out of town. I take a
morning ride there every day.' Then with a curt, 'Nice
doing business with you, Mr Stacey', he turned and
walked out of the saloon.

Before the saloon lamps had been lit Stacey had his
gang, six men, four of them 'breeds. Men who would
steal, with violence, from their own close kin to raise up
a little spending money. Before noon of the next day
he had told Frazer that he was ready to ride out and do
some burning down, if the price he had come up with
was accepted by the man with the money in Chicago.
His next meeting with Frazer was scheduled for two
days time. Stacey was waiting impatiently for the agent
to show up at the shack. He saw Frazer come riding in
and hoped he was bringing good news, or he would
have to pull up stakes in Bitter Water Springs as his
hired gunmen would shoot him for failing to come up
with the cash he had promised them. He was soon to

find out he was worrying for nothing.

'You can go ahead with the barn burning, Mr Stacey,' Frazer said without dismounting and, leaning down, handed Stacey a thick roll of dollar bills. 'Part now, the rest when my principal says so. The more farms burned down the bigger the final payment.' Seeing Stacey's disappointed scowl, he said, 'This is how business is conducted, Mr Stacey; the bill fully met, with bonuses, after the completion of the contract.' He gave a thin smile. 'Will you be giving your men the cash you promised them in one payment?'

Stacey had to admit the lawyer had a point. Pay the hard men he'd hired all they were due in one go he wouldn't see their asses for trail dust. He stuffed the bills into his coat pocket. 'We'll start up raidin' tonight, Mr Frazer.'

Now, Stacey thought angrily, he had to eat crow, tell Frazer that he would have to raise the price of the contract if he wanted him to continue with the raiding, or cut his boss's losses by calling off the deal. Five men killed had definitely shot up the hiring charges, it wasn't turning out to be easy money after all. He strode out of the saloon to meet up with Frazer and tell him the bad news thinking that even if Frazer turned him down he would hire a bunch of men himself and pay that farm another visit, in daytime, when the sodbuster least expected it and sweep across his piece of dirt burning and destroying everything in their path, including the sodbuster and his kin to kind of regain his shot-to-hell pride.

TWO

Judge Isaac Parker, Federal Judge of the Western District of Arkansas and whose jurisdiction also covered the wild lands of Indian Territory, looked across at Marshal Thomas Houseman standing at the other side of his desk. Never ceasing to wonder how a small built, elderly, grey-stubbled man, dressed in a dark store suit that shone with wear in patches like a mirror, topped by a battered plains hat, could be his number-one man hunter. A man who rode bold-assed, guns blazing into the outlaw hell holes in the Indian Territory with no more hesitation than a religous man would walk into a church meeting hall.

The judge had eyeballed desperadoes of all colours, white, brown, black, mixed bloods, even a yellow skinned Chinese man once, as he told them that he was going to have the pleasure seeing them hang on his six-rope gallows. Smiled back at them when they spat at him, dirty-mouthed him and heaped cursing death wishes on his person. But Marshal Houseman's unblinking-eyed stare that penetrated to his very soul, and gave the lie to his old man's washed-out appearance, was a gaze that gave him the shivers.

'Providing you're not hauling in a wagonload of prisoners when you come back in, Tom,' he said, 'I'd be obliged if you'd pay a visit to Bitter Water Springs and make contact with a farmer by the name of Adam Paxton. He's sent me a wire—'

'Bitter Water Springs is in the Cherokee Strip, Judge!' Houseman interrupted. 'Choctaw, Creek, Cree, and the rest of the so-called civilized tribes' land! They've got their own peace officers. You've got no jurisdiction there, Judge.'

Judge Parker smiled condescendingly at his marshal. 'I'm well aware of that discrepancy, Tom. But Mr Paxton's land is close to the Cherokee Strip's border so that puts him as near as damn in my bailiwick. A point I'm willing to debate with any lawman, lawyer or judge in the Strip.' The judge's smile became oilier. 'I'm sure that you will be most discreet when you cross over the line.'

Houseman scowled at the judge. 'Did this sodbuster let you know what his trouble is?'

'Night-rider trouble,' Judge Parker replied. 'They rode in to burn him out. But he must have beaten them off as he's still on his land. Now, I don't expect you to take on these raiders on your own, Tom. Just assess the situation. If you do discover that the men who are doing the burning out are holed-up near the line then, by hell, I'll raise a posse of twenty deputies and see them shot dead or hanged. Even if it means hot pursuing the no-good sonsuvbitches halfway across the Strip!'

'But I ain't got a deputy,' Marshal Houseman

growled bad-temperedly. 'Bein' that old Sam Peck caught a load of buckshot in his ass and other parts on the last trip out.'

'Yes, I'm well aware of that,' Judge Parker replied, thinking that it was unfortunate that Deputy Marshal Sam Peck, Marshal Houseman's tumbleweed wagon driver, had to pull up outside the jailhouse at Morganville just when the Pelham brothers, the men they were going to haul back to Fort Smith to dance on his gallows, burst out of the jail and peppered Sam with the shotgun's load they had grabbed from the sheriff after knifing him. Then the Pelham boys' luck had run out: Marshal Houseman shot the pair dead with his pistol faster that it takes to tell, robbing him of a dual hanging.

'I've hired a new marshal,' Judge Parker continued. 'A young boy, but keen to wear a lawman's badge. He's kin to Marshal Wallace who speaks highly of the boy. Told me he's more than a fair shot with a rifle.'

Marshal Houseman gave the judge an incredulous look. A young kid? More than a fair shot with a rifle? At what, he thought, varmints? The judge ought to know what it took to be a marshal in the lawless territory of the Nations. A land of bushwhackers and dry-gulchers. The son-of-a-bitch didn't give a hoot about his marshals getting shot up as long as they got the wanted men to swing on his gallows. Also kids tended to be yappy, and that was a trait he didn't like. Houseman reckoned that him and Sam Peck hadn't exchanged a couple of dozen words, not counting grunts and swear words, between them the whole year Sam had been his tumbleweed wagon driver. Which had suited both of their temperaments. And they whom they had served warrants on and brought back, chained up, to Fort Smith, weren't great talkers either. Their guns did the talking for them.

'Deputy Ezekiel Isaiah Butler ought to have the wagon ready for rolling out, Tom; he's keen to prove his worth,' Judge Parker added hurriedly wanting to pacify his po-faced marshal.

'Ezekeiel Isaiah!' Marshal Houseman blurted out. 'That's a handle for any man to be saddled with.' He narrowed-eyed the judge. 'The kid ain't one of these born-again Bible-preachin' characters, is he? He ain't aimin' to save my wicked soul while we're out there on the trail? If he is I'll drive the the damn wagon myself!'

Judge Parker smiled. 'Don't be so mean-minded, Tom, You must have been a young greenhorn once.' Though he doubted it. Men of Marshal Houseman's breed were born old, with the manhunter blood already flowing through their veins. The grumpy bastard probably cut his teeth on the barrel of a .45 Colt Peacemaker. Before he could say another word Marshal Houseman had swung round, muttering what he assumed to be curse words, and stomped out of his office. The judge winced as the door banged shut, the draught scattering the legal papers on his desk.

Judge Parker smiled again. Marshal Houseman was becoming more tetchy in his old age. Though he didn't think his late life tantrums would hinder the marshal in doing his job as a tracker down of wanted men.

Deputy Zeke Butler had hitched up the two mules and had seen to it that three days' supplies for them, and his horse, tied to the tailgate of the wagon, and Marshal Houseman's horse, plus rations for two men had been loaded on to the wagon. He was only waiting for his partner to show up to give the order to move out and he would be making his first trip as a genuine US Marshal. Zeke was both excited and worried, knowing that he was partner of a man not noted for his sociable disposition.

Marshal Houseman cast a sour-faced glance at the tall gangling youth standing by the wagon. He was dressed in homespun hand-me-downs. Whoever had worn the clothes last must have been a great deal shorter than his new deputy, who was showing several inches of bare ankles. Beneath a floppy-brimmed, well-stained hat, a wide-eyed face, that looked as though it didn't need the services of a razor, gazed dog-like pleading at him.

Marshal Houseman cursed Judge Parker under his breath. He was getting a backwoods hayseed as a deputy. He was about to enter the wild lands of the Nations with a boy who should be still behind a plough or feeding the hogs.

He was about to tell his deputy that it would have been in both their interests to have stayed on his pa's farm, but paused to take a closer look at his new deputy's horse.

It was a small, ridge-backed animal whose blood line must have included a freight wagon mule and an Indian war pony but whose coat shone with constant brushing and it had a contented well-fed look about it. The saddle gear was old, but had been painstakingly repaired. The leather was well waxed and the brass fittings sparkled in the sunlight. Marshal Houseman's attitude softened somewhat towards his partner.

A man who had the patience and the pride to look after his horse was a man, in his opinion, who would be willing to be taught how to stay alive so as to be able to bring in the wrongdoers for Judge Parker to pass sentence on. Still not acknowledging his deputy, Houseman keen-eyed the guns he was armed with. He was holding a battered-stocked, single load Sharps carbine. A gun he had fired at the rebs as they tried to storm the ridge above the Devil's Den at Gettysburg. The pistol the boy had tucked in the waistband of his pants looked another old-style weapon. A cap and ball Colt, he surmised. Which made him think that if they ever landed up in a gunfight the boy could get himself killed in the time it took to thumb a shell into the breech of his rifle or fit firing caps on his pistol reloads.

It was Zeke, who spoke first. 'We're ready to move out on your orders, Marshal,' he said. 'Once your gear's on the wagon,' he added apprehensively.

'Good,' Houseman replied curtly. He ran a quick-eyed check over the mules' traces and could see nothing to reprimand the boy for. The judge had been right, his new deputy could handle horses. 'But first,' he said, 'we'll go across to the stores and get you a Winchester repeater and a pistol that fires brass cartridges and a belt and holster. If that ancient cannon you've got stuffed in the top of your pants accidently discharges your voice will never break.'

They were about to move out, Deputy Butler sitting on the wagon seat ready to kick off the brake, Marshal

22

Houseman up on his horse. The marshal took a chew out of his pocket, took a bite out of it then offered the plug of tobacco to Zeke.

'No, thank you, Marshal,' Zeke said. 'It's against my beliefs to partake of tobacco and the demon drink.' He smiled nervously. 'Though I don't hold anything against any man who does smoke and drinks hard liquor.'

Marshal Houseman did some more silent cursing. Judge Parker could be hearing him singing hymns when he returned to Fort Smith. He suddenly had the uncomfortable feeling that maybe he wouldn't make it back. He hard-eyed his deputy.

'That's m'be so, Deputy Butler,' his voice as flinty as his gaze, 'but I hope your beliefs ain't against you pluggin' an outlaw who is hell bent on killin' the pair of us. Those fellas we hold warrants on are well past the "love thy neighbour" state. The sonsuvbitches are beyond redemption.'

Houseman saw his deputy stiffen and he was favoured with a reproachful look.

'Don't have any doubts about me not doin' my duty, Marshal Houseman,' Zeke said firm-voiced. 'I have never killed a man before but I would not hesitate to do so if our lives were in danger. I believe what the Old Testament says, that a man should smite his enemies hip and thigh. Those men are thieves, killers, doing Satan's work here on earth. They—'

The marshal raised a protesting hand. He didn't need a would-be preacher telling him that the men he hauled into Fort Smith to stand trail were sinners of some repute. Though he had to admit that when he had shot the Pelham boys it didn't occur to him that he had 'smote' them down.

'OK, Deputy,' he said. 'I believe you. Now let's go and get this wagon full of those sinners roamin' around out there.'

As they crossed the line into the Nations, Marshal Houseman found himself worrying more about his deputy's opinion of him than the dangers he knew that lay ahead. He was already in the boy's black book for chewing the tobacco weed. When he discovered that he took a regular pull at the whiskey bottle in his saddle-bag, just to ease the aches and the chills of a cold night camp, he'd be well on the road to perdition. He would be beyond redemtion if Deputy Butler found out that he often visited the widow, Mrs Hedgepath, who ran a boarding-house in White Oaks to ease his lewd sins of the flesh.

THREE

Kalvin S. Striker, an all-round big man, managing director and sole shareholder of the Indian Territory Land Development Company, eyeballed his prospective new backers sitting round his desk in his office in Chicago. He was desperate to get hold of some of the hard-faced, penny-counting bastards' cash or he would go bust and his hope of becoming a big land wheeler-dealer magnate would be ended. His operation in the Cherokee Strip was costing a great deal more cash than he had bargained for. Not only would he be broke but could end up in jail if the law ever found out just how illegal his company was doing business in the territory. It was make or break time for him.

Striker fixed his heavy-jowled face into a skin-deep look of confidence of a man whose company was going places fast.

'Gentlemen,' he began, his voice oozing with the same confidence. 'You may have heard already that there's a move from the government to open up the whole of the Indian Territory, that includes the Cherokee Strip, for development. Selling parcels of land, at a fixed price, on a first come, first served basis, a section per man or family. So that puts land developers like me and you, gentlemen, out of business.'

'Then why are you asking us to put up our hard-earned cash if we can't get hold of a sizeable piece of real estate?' one of the businessmen asked.

Striker did his fixed grin routine again. 'That's a fair point, Mr Chandler, it's only right you should make sure that you are not being conned into parting with your cash so I'll put your minds at rest. The restriction on the purchasing of land only applies to the new settlers. There's nothing to stop a real estate developer from buying land already being worked from the owner. And that's what I've been doing for the last few months, buying land from the Cree, Cherokee and other Indian homesteaders. Some of our civilized red brethen don't take to being farmers. Hard cash on the barrel head is a great temptation for them to quit their holdings. Then they can indulge in their pet vices of gambling and drinking.'

Striker, sensing that he had the hard-faced land speculators' interest, carried on with his sales pitch.

'And I'm talking about a lot of holdings here, gentlemen. When the government gives the go-ahead for the Cherokee Strip land sale, the biggest of its kind ever, there'll be thousands of newly arrived immigrants in New York and Boston and other such ports, seeking a piece of growing land that they craved for back there in the old country. They'll have scraped up enough cash to buy their dream. But there'll not be enough good, well-watered land to accommodate them all. That's when the Indian Territory Land Development

Company steps in.' Striker gave an all-toothed wolfish grin. 'Desperate men will pay a desperate price to get what they have journeyed all this way for.'

Striker heard a general stirring of asses on seats. The prospect of easy, no risk big returns on their capital had the money-grabbing bastards hooked. He sat back and let them mentally chew over the prospect he had pictured for them. The men sitting at the table were hard wheeler-dealers and they could sniff out a con two states distance away. It wouldn't do to oversell himself.

It was the doubter, Chandler who spoke. 'If it's such a good money-making scheme as you've told us, why cut us in? Why don't you keep it all for yourself?'

Striker showed his serious-faced businessman's look. 'That's a fair point, Chandler,' he said. 'Keeping the company in my own hands would make me a considerable amount of money but, like you, gentlemen, I want a big killing. That means buying up all the land I can get and I haven't got the capital to do it. The capital I require must be raised quickly. The government could announce at any time the date of the proposed land sale then other land developers could show up in the territory and that would up the price of the strips of land I'm trying to buy.'

Striker judged it was time to put his proposal to the vote. 'I think that I've talked enough, gentlemen,' he said. 'I'll leave it to you to show in the usual manner whether you are in or out. It's a money-making scheme that only comes once in a lifetime.'

Four right hands shot up in the air, Chandler's a little slower than the other three.

Striker got to his feet, smiling. 'Good, gentlemen,'

he said. 'You won't regret your decision. While my business manager draws up the relevant papers we can enjoy a cigar and some excellent Scotch in the other office.'

Striker's make-believe smile was to hide his gut-chewing worry that the Indian Territory Land Development Company had just been hit by big, unexpected trouble. If the four who were drinking his single malt and smoking his expensive cigars knew that their company employed men to burn out and generally harass Indian land owners until they were pleased to get rid of their holdings at any price, he wouldn't see a red cent of their money. Striker was a firm believer that the means justifies the big payoff at the end. Though, by the urgent wire he had just received from Frazer, the means didn't seem to be working.

Frazer had stated in the flimsy that higher costs must be met if the enterprise is to continue. Higher costs! Strikers' smile almost slipped. He had been given to understand that in the so-called 'wild' West there was an abundance of men who would cut their grandmothers' throats for a few dollars. He would have to make the long journey to Bitter Water Springs and sort out the hold up of the operation himself. He'd be damned if he was going to waste his newly raised cash unless it was absolutely necessary. The sooner he ushered his partners out of the office, without giving the impression that he was turfing them out, the sooner he would be on the train heading south, ending with a ball-aching trip by stage to Bitter Water Springs.

FOUR

Much to Marshal Houseman's surprise his new deputy wasn't a blabbermouth. Deputy Butler sat on the wagon seat as shut-faced as an Indian. And he was forced to admit, albeit grudgingly, that Marshal Wallace had told the truth about his nephew's capabilities, the boy could handle a mule team as good as any man he knew, and they were a pair of wall-eyed, ornery sons-of-bitches.

Zeke wasn't showing the excitement he was feeling being the partner of Judge Parker's top lawman. He gave an inner grin. Though the old buzzard wasn't much of a talker, even when back along the trail a piece he had swung down from his horse and sat alongside him on the seat, Zeke noticed that the marshal wasn't sitting relaxed. He held his rifle across his knees, jaws working on his chaw, as he kept an eye-swivelling watch on both sides of the trail. Which made him realize that he wasn't on a hay ride and had to be alert as the marshal.

He ceased his daydreaming. A no-good sinner could be hunkered down behind some rock round the next bend in the trail ready to draw a bead on them with his rifle. Slowly, so as not to let Marshal Houseman know that he'd been neglecting his duty, he eased his pistol an inch or two out of its holster. He had never taken part in a gunfight before, but he was of the opinion that the man who had the edge was the man who shot first. Then as hawk-eyed as the marshal he scanned ahead of them confident on seeing any movement in the long grass or clumps of brush he would know if it was caused by the wind, a critter, or a man waiting in ambush.

'Pull up, Deputy!' Marshal Houseman said. 'We'll make camp by that stream there. It'll be dark soon and it ain't wise to travel along this stretch of the trail in bad light.' He grinned when he saw the alarmed look on Zeke's face. 'Don't fret yourself, boy, it ain't that we're likely to be bushwhacked. It's just from here to the Canadian the way ain't laid out like some regular turnpike. It's full of potholes and ruts and more than likely we'd shed a wheel, or worse, break an axle.' He grinned again. 'Then by heck we could be haulin' back any wanted men we collect on the flat bed of a farm wagon – if we can persuade a sodbuster to hire one out.'

By the time Zeke had unhitched the mules, unsaddled the horses and led them down the stream to water them, and rub them down, all without orders from the marshal, Houseman had a dry kindling fire going with a soot-encrusted coffeee pot hanging over the flames coming up to the boil, and was opening a can of beans to warm up in an equally fire scorched pan. The coffee and beans, and some hard biscuits would be their fare

30

for the night, the marshal thankful that he had brought the whiskey to ease the griping pains the beans inflicted on his innards.

Zeke came up to the fire saying that he had corn fed the horses and mules and had hobbled them for the night.

'Good,' replied Houseman. Then seeing his deputy's curled-up nose look as he eyed their supper he said, almost apologetically, 'I know it ain't much of a repast, Deputy, after a hard day's trailin' but we'll make up for it at the widow Hedgepath's eating-house at White Oaks the far-side of the Canadian.'

'Make the coffee, Marshal!' Zeke said, with some authority in his voice. 'And take the beans off before you burn them. I've a parcel of decent chow in my saddle-bags. Pa rode into Fort Smith and gave it to me as I was hitchin' up the mules.'

Marshal Houseman was somewhat taken aback at the sudden bossy turn in his deputy's character to do anything but carry out his orders, take the beans off the fire and make the coffee.

Zeke strode back to the fire with a shiny clean skillet held in one hand and a tarpaper-wrapped parcel in the other. He squatted down at the fire and laid the frying pan on a flaming log. Carefully unwrapping the paper bundle he took out several slices of thick sliced sow belly and dropped them into the pan. When the bacon fat began to sizzle and spread over the bottom of the pan he took out four eggs from the parcel, expertly cracked them and dropped them alongside the bacon.

A drooling-mouthed Marshal Houseman watched his deputy at work shifting the eggs around the pan with the slickness of a fancy hotel's chef, and man enough to admit he had judged the kid too quickly back there at Fort Smith. He was definitely no free-loader. And also man enough to say, 'That smells real good, Deputy. Better than just a mess of beans.'

'Heat those beans up again, Marshal,' Zeke said. 'And grab your plate, this is about ready to dish out.'

A well-fed Marshal Houseman sat with his back against a rock, drawing contently at his pipe. He'd had a quick pull at the whiskey while his deputy was at the stream washing the plates and pans, telling him before he left the fire to do the chores that he had always been told that cleanliness came next to Godliness. The marshal grinned, the easy come by smile of a living like a hog, and liking it, old sinner.

When Zeke came up from the stream he laid the cooking utensils by the fire then sat down opposite the marshal. Houseman could see the pride in his deputy's face at being able to prove that he could pull his weight on the trail. Though he had yet to prove his worth in a gunfight the marshal realized that it would be down-right churlish of him not to accept the fact that the boy had the makings of a good US marshal in him and he had to treat him as such. He told him about Judge Parker asking him to check out some raiders operating in the Cherokee Strip.

'Now what lawbreakin' is goin' on in that territory ain't exactly our business, Deputy, it's beyond our remit,' he said. 'But old Parker takes it kinda personal if he hears of law breakin' in the whole of the Nations.' He grinned. 'He ain't gone to all that expense havin'' that six-man gallows built just to stand idle, but we ain't wastin' a lot of our time in the Strip. There's plenty of bad-asses, beggin' your pardon, Deputy, lawbreakers, in our bailiwick.'

He favoured his deputy with what he hoped was a fatherly concerned look before speaking again. 'Now I must warn you about those fellas we could be haulin' back to stand trial at Judge Parker's court. They'll gaze at you with hard-done-by looks as though there's shafts of righteousness shinin' out of their butts, but take no heed of them. They're the last of the holdouts, live their lives by the use of their guns. Gettin' their where-withal any way but by honestly raised sweat. Turn your back on them and you're a dead man. Tomorrow we'll make it to the Canadian, but instead of crossin' it we'll make a detour along the river to pay a call on Mrs Belle Starr at Younger's Bend.'

'Mrs Belle Starr, Marshal? Who is she?' asked a curious-eyed Zeke.

Marshal Houseman grinned. 'She's a lady that runs a sorta guest house for owlhoots from as far away as Kansas and Missouri. Most of the lawbreakin' that goes on hereabouts Belle will have say in it, or at least know about it. The men who are doin' the raidin' in the Strip will be a sizeable bunch of riders. Belle oughta have intelligence about a new gang operatin' in the Strip.' He grinned. 'That's if she can go agin her natural law-breakin' instincts by talkin' to a marshal.' Houseman gave a deep sigh. 'Now it's about time we turned in for the night, Deputy, I ain't as young as was.'

Zeke, keen to show his commitment as a peace officer, asked the marshal if he wanted him to stand the first watch.

Houseman laughed. 'There ain't no need for either of us to lose any sleep, Deputy,' he said. 'Josh, that old horse of mine, has a mean streak in him. He'll raise hell, stompin' his feet and hollerin' no end if any man, critter, or whatever comes within a hundred yards of this camp.' Then he laid down his blanket and, with a gruff 'Good night, Deputy', he rolled on to his side. With a full belly and the whiskey still warm inside him he soon dropped off to sleep.

It was a while before Zeke relaxed enough to get stretched out on his bedroll; worrying doubts were nagging at him. He opined he had come through his first day as a US marshal OK and that Marshal Houseman's first opinions of him had softened somewhat. What was chewing away at him was whether he would be able to draw his pistol and shoot down a fellow Christian, even a back-sliding one. He had told the marshal that he would not hesitate in meting out the ultimate retribution to black-hearted sinners. But he was no fiery-blooded Old Testament zealot who slew his enemies by the sword, slingshot, or the jawbone of a critter. He could only trust that when the moment of truth came the Good Lord would not let him be found wanting. Then, trying not to fret any more about his misgivings, he built up the fire for the night and rolled out his blanket. Saying a short, but fervent, prayer, he laid down and tried to get some sleep.

Houseman groaned and opened his eyes. Hard ground beds were ageing him fast. He caught the mouth-watering smell of bacon frying and freshly boiled coffee and sat up with a jerk. He saw his deputy, back towards him sitting on his heels busy at the fire, and, to his surprise, the mules were hitched up to the wagon. The kid must have been up well before first light. And he had been worried about carrying a passenger. Cursing under his breath he got to his feet.

'You should have woken me up, Deputy,' he growled, embarrassed as he joined Zeke at the fire. 'There ain't no need for you to do all the chores.' He bleary-eyed his deputy. 'Don't you sodbusters need sleep?'

Zeke grinned at him. 'Not much, Marshal. By now me and my pa would have planted the big field. Chow's ready when you are.'

Houseman quickly bundled up his bedroll then reached into his saddle-bag and took out a lump of yellow soap and a once white frayed-ended towel. 'I'll go and freshen up first, Deputy.' He couldn't remember ever washing before so early in the day. Some of the kid's goodness must be rubbing off on him. 'Once we've eaten and fed the horses we can be on our way.'

'The horses have been fed, Marshal,' replied Zeke.

And Marshal Houseman reckoned he had been well and truly put in his place.

'Pa allus insisted that horses and the stock had to be fed before we ate, Marshal,' Zeke said. 'He said they were also God's creatures.'

Houseman was out of his depth. Though, like his deputy, he saw to it that his horse was regularly watered and fed it was for purely down to earth reasons, like saving his hide. It wouldn't be in his best interests to be up on a half-starved horse if forced into a tight corner by a bunch of owlhoots. That horses and cows were also God's creatures had never entered his head at all. He had enough occupying his mind thinking of how he could get the jump on some of God's two-legged critters, the killing, sinning kind. But to show appreciation of his deputy's usefulness he said, 'You're fittin' in well, Zeke.'

Zeke smiled proudly as he watched the marshal walking down to the stream. He could wear his badge with confidence. And he had no doubts now that if either of their lives were at risk he would not hesitate to kill to protect them.

FIVE

A wary-eyed Mrs Belle Starr standing on her front porch watched the tumbleweed wagon and its accompanying rider come splashing across the ford. She muttered an unlady-like curse as she recognized the rider, Marshal Houseman, Judge Parker's number-one bloodhound. For years she and Houseman had been playing a cat and mouse game. He would show up out of the blue hoping to rope in any of her owlhoot visitors he held warrants on. Plans to rob a certain bank, or lift some rancher's cows, plans worked out in her own front parlour, had to be abandoned until the planners knew that Marshal Houseman was long gone, to cast the 'Hanging' Judge's fearsome presence by proxy on other lawbreakers in the territory.

Her smile as the wagon and Houseman drew up in front of her porch was as sincere as a snake-oil salesman's. It became somewhat genuine when she got a good look at the deputy driving the wagon. 'Is old Parker runnin' short of cash, Marshal, that he can't afford to hire grown men as deputies?' she said. 'He isn't your boy, is he?' she added mockingly.

Houseman's smile was as false as Belle's. Ignoring her remarks about his deputy he touched the brim of his hat in greeting and growled a curt, 'Ma'am.'

He cast a quick glance at the horse corral. No bunch of raiders was staying at Younger's Bend. Only four horses were in the stockade, one, he opined, belonging to the man standing in the far end of the porch. The man stepped out of the shadows and Houseman got a clear sighting of him. Though he was wearing a store suit, by the look of his all bone face he wouldn't have looked out of place wearing a breech clout with a couple of feathers stuck in his hair. On its own accord his hand slipped down to the butt of his pistol.

'If that Injun-faced fella so much as breaks wind you put him down,' he hissed. 'Can you do that, Deputy Butler?'

Zeke was red-faced at Belle's jibe but he still goggle-eyed her. He had never seen a female with a pistol strapped around her waist before. She was only a small-built woman, thinner than his ma, wearing a colourful patterned dress that reached to the toes of her spurred riding boots. And she sported a big wide-brimmed hat that had more feathers sticking out of it than the rear end of a turkey cock. When Belle lifted her head and he got a good look at the drawn hard, mannish face Zeke didn't doubt that the pistol she wore wasn't for show. She would use it with good effect if she had to. He prayed it would not be aimed at him. He had only just convinced himself that he could fire back at some owlhoot: he'd never thought that he might have to face a female lawbreaker. That unnerving possiblity would cause him more sleepless nights.

Zeke dragged his gaze off Mrs Belle Starr and on to
the man the marshal had told him to kill if forced to.
He swallowed hard. 'Yeah, Marshal,' he said with more
confidence than he was feeling. Slowly he wiped the
sweat off his gun hand.

'I'd be obliged if I could have word with you in
private, Belle,' Houseman said. He was talking to Belle
but gimlet-eyeing the door and the window. The stone-
faced dude could have one or two friends with him and
if they were calling at Younger's Bend they'd be men
wanted by the law in someplace or other. Men who, to
save their dirty hides, would gun down a couple of
marshals. Though when he did risk a quick look at
Belle he could see no signs of tension in her face. So it
didn't look as though he and the boy had ridden unexpectedly into a tight corner, though that didn't mean
they had to relax their vigilance.

The sharp discharge of a pistol, a sharper howl of
pain from the man on the porch caused Houseman to
jump ass in his saddle with alarm. His pistol was fisted,
fully cocked, aimed in the general direction of the
window and the door. He glared angrily at Belle. 'Are
there any more of the sonsuvbitches inside!' he yelled,
glancing at the bent-over man clutching at his right
shoulder.

'He's on his own!' a frantic-looking Belle cried. 'I
never set up this situation, honest, Marshal. I've never
clapped eyes on the asshole before today. He said he
hailed from Missouri!'

Some of Houseman's embarrassed anger at being
caught off guard died away. Again he was man enough
to admit that if his deputy hadn't been sharp-eyed it

could have been him holding a busted shoulder, or worse. Deputy Ezekiel Isaiah Butler was learning the marshalling business fast, and good.

He kneed his horse closer to the porch until he was gazing down at the pain-racked-faced, dirty-mouthing man. 'You may not think so right now, Missouri,' he grated, 'but you're lucky on two counts. Number one, that my deputy is a Christian-minded boy and he was charitable enough to only wing you when I gave him strict orders to kill you if you made a move against us. Secondly, I ain't got the time to haul you back to Fort Smith and have old George Maledon, Parker's hangman, slip one of his hemp collars around your dirty neck.' He hard-eyed Belle. 'See to his wound so he can get on his way buck to Missouri before I change my mind and have me a lynchin'. Then we'll have that chat.'

The wounded man spat a stream of curses at him. Houseman cold-smiled. 'Curb that language. Missouri, or Belle might take offence and not fix up that shoulder.'

He turned his horse round and walked it back to the wagon where Zeke was still holding his pistol on the man he had wounded.

'Sharp work, Deputy,' he said. 'He fooled me. I never thought that he'd be so desperate as to take on two marshals. He must have a whole heap of warrants posted on him up there in Missouri.'

'But I didn't kill him, Marshal,' Zeke replied. 'At the last minute I only winged him.'

'That don't matter,' Houseman said. 'You stopped him from killin' us. And it'll be a long spell before he can use a pistol with that arm. I'll keep an eye on him while Belle fixes him up then I'll send him on his way. Then I'll have that talk with her to see if she can be of any help to us. I'd be obliged if you'd water the horses so we can get on the trail to Bitter Water Springs. We don't want to stay around here, Deputy, in case a whole bunch of owlhoots from Missouri comes bowlin' in.'

The trail dust of the patched-up Missourian had long since settled, but Zeke, after he had watered the animals, kept a grim-faced watch from the porch on the two trails that led to the house though he was still somewhat jangled nerved. He had told the marshal that he would not hesitate to use his pistol in the line of duty, but hearing the man he had shot shriek with pain had been more gut churning than he had imagined. Inside the house he heard the marshal telling Mrs Belle Starr the reason for their visit.

'There hasn't been any bunches of riders showing up here, Marshal,' Belle said. 'The men who pay me a call are generally loners, or men running gangs in Kansas or Missouri. I reckon if a man wanted to raise a gang of owlhoots across there in the Strip he would find all the men he'd need within spitting distance of where he was standing.' Wanting to get Houseman searching for the raiders well away from Younger's Bend so she and her husband, Blue Duck, could continue with their lawless activities she broke her natural born code by passing on information regarding the whereabout of lawbreakers she'd had contacts with to a US marshal.

'There was a fella who passed by here a few days ago,

41

heading for Kansas,' she said, 'who told me that he had been riding with some other hard men bossed over by a fella called Stacey, Bitter Water Springs way. Whether it's the bunch you're looking for I don't rightly know. He didn't tell what business Stacey hired him for. All I know is that he quit the outfit as things had got too hot for him to handle.'

Houseman gave a twitch of a grin. Bitter Water Springs was close by the farm that had been raided. They weren't riding into the Strip blindfolded, they had a name. And coming to Younger's Bend had got his deputy blooded as a lawman. His face boned over, and found him not so sharp-eyed as he might have been.

'Thanks for your information, Belle,' he said. 'I'm sorry about the upset on your front porch.'

'That's OK, Marshal,' Belle replied. 'It wasn't of your making; the asshole chose how to play it.'

Houseman gave a slight goodbye nod then got to his feet and walked out of the house.

Belle watched them leave saying a silent prayer that Marshal Houseman would get himself gunned down by the men he was tracking. Then she would have no problem keeping Younger's Bend an open house for the wild, sharpshooting, Kansas backwoods boys. But being a sinful woman who consorted with lawless men she didn't expect her prayers to be answered.

SIX

'Let's hope that Sheriff Parson ain't holdin' any men with Fort Smith issue warrants on them, Deputy,' Houseman said, as they came into White Oaks. 'Or he'll have to keep them in his cells until we've done what I told you the judge asked me to do, check out the night raidin' that's goin' on across there in the Strip.' Houseman spat between his horses's ears. 'Though as I said, we ain't goin' to do a lot of snoopin' around. To hell with the judge's orders; our job is to take wanted men back to Fort Smith to stand trail for their wrong-doin's.'

Zeke drew the wagon up outside the sheriff's office and jumped down from the seat and began easing the belly straps on the mules, an action that earned him another plus point from Houseman as he dismounted.

After Houseman had exchanged a few words of greeting to two passers by the pair of them walked into the office. The marshal introduced Zeke to Sheriff Bob Parson, a small, bulky, more-fat-than-muscle man, who was sitting half-dozing in a chair behind his desk. Houseman grinned at Zeke. 'Huntin' down bad-asses in this neck of the woods sure tires a man out, Deputy.'

The sheriff sat up with a jerk and gave them a bleary-eyed look. 'Oh, it's you, Tom. I wasn't expectin' you rollin' in this early.'

Houseman noticed the lawman casting a eyebrow-raised look at his deputy and saw Zeke's face redden with embarrassment.

'I know what you're thinkin', Bob,' he said, 'that Deputy Butler here is a mite young to be wearin' a marshal's badge. But don't let his youthful appearance fool you any. Back there at Belle Starr's robbers' roost he outshot a Missouri brush boy, saved me from gettin' plugged.'

Zeke tightened his face and gave the sheriff a narrow-eyed hard-man's stare, or so he believed. He had the satisfaction of seeing a look of respect show on the peace officer's face.

With a muttered, 'Yeah, well', and a clearing of his throat, the sheriff switched his gaze back on to Marshal Houseman. He jerked a thumb over his shoulder. 'Johnny Bear Paw is back there waitin' for you to take him to Fort Smith.'

'Bear Paw?' said a surprised Houseman. 'I ain't holdin' any papers on that Injun, Sheriff! Why, he's the town drunk! Nearly every time I call here that Injun's in one of your cells sleepin' off a session of downin' the fire water. Judge Parker will have my balls if I haul a drunkard into his court. Let him lie there till he sleeps it off as you normally do. Then have him do some chores about the place to pay for his chow.'

'That's what I usually do with the drunken bum,' Sheriff Parson replied. 'But this time when Bear Paw

44

was liquored up he stabbed a fella, well, it weren't no more than a scratch, but the way Madison, straw boss of the YW cattle spread, tells it, Bear Paw was all set to lift his hair.'

'Was he?' Houseman asked.

'Naw,' replied the sheriff. 'Bear Paw was tangle-footin' his way along the boardwalk waving his knife about when Madison came out of the saloon and barged into him and accidently got his shirt sleeve and arm cut.' The sheriff gave a derisive snort. 'I've shed more blood shavin'. But Madison is a nasty piece of work. The hard-nosed bastard yanked out his pistol and cold-cocked Bear Paw, then started bootin' him as he lay on the ground. If one of my deputy's hadn't shown up, Bear Paw would have been downin' his next shot of fire water in his happy huntin' grounds. Madison and some of his crew are liquorin' themselves up in the saloon. If I turn Bear Paw loose he could be headin' for another beatin' up, if not today then some other day as long as he stays around town. Madison ain't a forgivin' man.'

'Yeah, I see your point, Bob,' replied Houseman. 'Now hear mine. The judge got a wire from a Mr Paxton, a sodbuster near Bitter Water Springs tellin' him that his farm had been raided and wanted his help to rope in the raiders. Now the old goat wants me to kinda sneak across the line to try and find out what I can about the raiders in territory I ain't got the author-ity of my badge to back me up!' Scowling, he sharp-eyed the sheriff. 'You ain't seen a bunch of strange faces in town, Bob?'

Sheriff Parson shook his head. 'The only bunches of

men I've seen are the ranch crews ridin' in on pay day.' Po-faced he added, 'Just to cheer you up, Tom, the Paxton farm ain't the only place that's been raided. Several Indian holdin's have been put to the torch. Though the raidin' could have ended as Paxton and his family shot down five of the sonsuvbitches.'

Houseman's face paled. For Zeke's sake he held back his curses. 'There seems to be big trouble brewin' across there in the Strip. I told the judge it was too big a task for us to handle. It's the peace officers in the Strip's problem not mine, or the judge's. But Parker gets kinda worked up when he hears of wrongdoers he can't get his hands on.'

Sheriff Parson grinned again. 'If you sober up Bear Paw, him bein' a full-blood Injun an' all, he could do some trackin' for you. Like pickin' up the trail of what's left of the night hawks.'

Again, only the presence of his Holy Joe deputy stopped Houseman from cursing the sheriff. 'By what I've heard tell of that Injun,' he snarled, 'if you opened his cell door, him needin' a call of nature, he would be hard pressed to find his way to the crapper!'

'But we can't leave him here in White Oaks, Marshal, It's – it's not Christian like,' Zeke said, speaking for the first time. 'His death would be on our hands.'

Houseman cast a jaundiced-eye glare at Zeke. He had lived with death on his hands, head, wherever, for twice as long as he deputy had been drawing breath.

'We ain't rolling into the strip with the tumbleweed wagon, Deputy,' he said. 'The judge said we've to go pussy-footin' in. You drivin' in the wagon would let the whole territory know that we're the hanging judge's marshals. And that, Deputy Butler, will cause one hell of an upset with the local lawmen. And send any lawbreaker runnin' for cover till we move on. And I'll have to tell Parker that our mission was a failure. And believe me, boy, he won't take kindly to hearin' that.'

There was another reason why Houseman didn't want to be saddled with a prisoner, especially one he held no warrant on; he needed to do some sneaking about here in town, such as paying a call on the widow Hedgepath before heading for the Strip to indulge in what his deputy would call sinful lusting of the flesh, the fine looking widow's flesh.

'I can keep an eye on him, Marshal,' Zeke said. 'He can't get hold of any of the Devil's drink on the trail so he could be, as Sheriff Parson stated, of some help in readin' likely sign.'

For a few fleeting, confused seconds Sheriff Parson thought he was sitting in on a church revival meeting hearing words such as, the 'Devil's drink' and 'Christian like' from Houseman's young deputy. The kid had got religion real bad. But the kid was wrong in thinking that Bear Paw wouldn't be able to get his hands on any strong liquor on the trail. He'd bet his bottom dollar that Houseman had a bottle of the demon drink, whiskey for preference, in one of his saddle-bags. He grinned to himself. Taking into account Houseman's other sinful pastime, as the kid would see it, pleasuring the widow Hedgepath, the kid didn't know just how sinful a partner he had.

'It's a good idea your deputy's come up with, Tom,' he said. 'You only need to take Bear Paw across the line then turn him loose. Him bein' a Cherokee he's bound to have some of his kin farmin' nearby.'

Houseman thought a while about the sheriff's suggestion before giving a grunted, 'Yeah, yeah, I reckon we could do that. It'll mean extra work for you, Deputy, but you seem all for it. You drive the wagon along to the feed barn, just along the street apiece, and tell Murphy, he's the owner, to keep it and the mules in his barn for few days. Then ask him to hire you a horse, just a horse, no saddle gear. Bear Paw will have to remember how he once rode a pony bare-assed. Tell Murphy I'll settle up with him before we leave.' Houseman lowered his head sheepishly. 'I've, er, some urgent business to see to in town. I'll meet up with you outside here in a about a coupla hours or so. OK?'

'OK, Marshal,' replied Zeke, eager to be trusted by Houseman to work on his own again.

Houseman gave Sheriff Parson a shifty-eyed look. 'You'd better keep Bear Paw locked in his cell, Bob, until we're ready to move out. Just in case Madison and his crew are still in town and lookin' for trouble.'

'I'll do that, Tom,' the sheriff said. Smirking he added, 'You go and see to that "urgent" business' you mentioned. I hope it goes good for you.'

Houseman cast him a scowling backwards glance as he walked out of the office.

SEVEN

Houseman and Zeke, with Bear Paw trailing behind them, rode out of White Oaks, Zeke opining that the business Marshal Houseman had to see to must have definitely worked out in his favour. He was sure the marshal was smiling, or as near to smiling as his stone-faced visage was capable of. And he was a mite disappointed that, owing to the urgency to get Bear Paw out of town before he was the cause of any more trouble, he'd not had the chance to partake of the fine cooked food that Mrs Hedgepath served up in her eating-house. But, as a peace officer, Zeke accepted that duty came first.

He glanced over his shoulder at Bear Paw. He'd never had close dealings with an Indian before but he had heard his pa's neighbours call them bloodthirsty savages. Sagging on his horse like a burst feed sack Mr Bear Paw looked anything but wild and fearsome.

Bear Paw was suffering the craving agonies of three liquorless days plus the added aches and pains of the beating he had taken from Madison. Every time his horse put a foot to the ground it jerked at his nerve ends causing him to give a stifled un-Indian groan of pain. Right now Bear Paw wished he was dead. Then an icy-cold thought broke through his misery. If the two marshals were not escorting him out of town the white-eyed dog, Madison would grant that wish. Then as sober as he had been for a long time Bear Paw asked himself if he really wanted to die. Was it written in the Book of Life that the Cherokee, Bear Paw, son of Chief Hawk Face, was to die from drinking white-eyes' whiskey before his fortieth summer?

Bear Paw had blood kin of his father's in the Strip but he couldn't see them feeding and housing a distant relative who slept off his drunkeness lying in the street of some white man's town like a cur dog even out of respect to his dead father. If he didn't change his way of existing – Bear Paw knew it wasn't living – he could anger another white man and meet the same fate he had narrowly escaped in White Oaks in the Cherokee Strip.

He had to end his craving for whiskey if he wanted to stay alive, as from now, act with the dignity of his father's blood line. And that, Bear Paw reasoned, was going to be one big battle. Then, experiencing some degree of pride in his race, he straightened up on his horse.

Zeke eased back his horse until Bear Paw caught up with him, then he had a closer look at the face of the man who was his first prisoner as a deputy marshal. Bear Paw couldn't be all that old, he thought, but the slow poison of the demon whiskey had marked his face with the haggard lines of a man older than his years. A man, by his appearance, who was living through his own personal hell, figuring that Indians believed in hell. He slipped his canteen off his saddle horn and offered it to Bear Paw.

Grinning he said, 'You look as though you could do with a drink, Mr Bear Paw.'

Bear Paw managed a ghost of a smile. Before he had made his promise to quit drinking he firmly believed, being so desperate for a drink, he would have lifted the young boy's hair to get his lips around the neck of a whiskey bottle, now he had to make do with water and, it was kindly given. He gave a muttered, 'Thanks', and took hold of the canteen.

Houseman twisted in his saddle and looked back at his deputy. 'We'll make camp here alongside that crick,' he said. 'Accordin' to the sheriff if we follow it eastwards we'll make Mr Paxton's farm. I reckon night will be cuttin' in by then and it wouldn't be wise for us to be payin' an unexpected call on a family that's just had a shoot-out with a bunch of marauders.'

After the three of them had dismounted, Zeke soon had a fire going with a dixie of water hotting up for the coffee. Bear Paw, to take his mind off the craving for a nerve calming shot of whiskey, offered to see that the horses were watered at the creek. Houseman, sitting relaxed at the fire drawing on his pipe, was still savouring the blood-coursing feel of the widow Hedgepath's soft, warm flesh.

While he was ankle deep in the water Bear Paw, trying to think of positive thoughts about his future, caught a smell of himself: a throat-gagging stink of rancid sweat and dried vomit and bloodstained clothes, strong enough to send a skunk running for cover.

Gingerly he began to strip off his clothes.

A grinning Houseman looked across the fire at Zeke as he heard the splashing in the creek. 'That Injun could be fightin' his demon, Deputy,' he said. 'By the smell of him bathin' ain't been a regular habit of his. Just as well. I would have thrown him in that crick before I'd let him share the fire.' He took a couple of sucks at his pipe before speaking again. 'Bear Paw ain't really our prisoner, Deputy; we're only obligin' the sheriff, savin' him from an awkward situation. I could send him on his way, but more than likely he'll try and head for the nearest gin palace and that will be in White Oaks. So I guess we'll have to nursemaid him until we get to the Strip.' Though that situation didn't go down well with him at all.

In his .saddle-bag was his nightcap bottle of whiskey. He could sneak out the bottle and have a quick pull at it behind his deputy's back, but in no way could he risk pulling it out in the presence of an Indian who, for the last couple of years, had been smelling out where his next shot of fire water was coming from.

'M'be you should take a blanket to Bear Paw, Deputy,' he said. 'He'll be feelin' kinda chilly steppin' outa that crick jaybird naked with all that dirt washed off him.' He reached behind him. 'Here, take mine, I'll see to the coffee,' he said, and tossed the blanket across to Zeke.

Zeke picked it up and got to his feet. 'I'll tie up the horses for the night as well, Marshal,' he said. 'Then Bear Paw can come straight up to the fire.'

As he hurried down to the creek a pleasantly surprised Zeke was thinking that the milk of human kindness showed up in the most unlikely of sinners.

The 'sinner' was opening his saddle-bag and reaching for the whiskey. Being that it was some time before his deputy returned, Houseman had time to have two pulls at the bottle.

'Any trouble with Bear Paw or the horses, Deputy?' Houseman asked, as Zeke came back to the fire. 'You've been gone a mite longer than I expected, the coffee will want heatin' up again.'

'No, everything's OK, Marshal,' replied Zeke, as he set the coffee pot back on the fire. 'Bear Paw washed his clothes as well and being that's all the clothes he's got he can't put them back on till they've dried. I've lit him a fire in a small cave in the rock face on the other side of the crick where he can dry them out faster than standin' in front of this fire. And he thanked you for the loan of the blanket, Marshal. When the coffee comes to the boil I'll take him a mugful.' Zeke gave Houseman a weighing-up look and saw a tired-faced elderly man. 'I'll stand the first watch,' he added.

Houseman was tired. His hectic session with the widow Hedgepath, and his generous swigs at the whiskey were making it an effort to keep his eyes open.

'You do that, Deputy,' he said, hoping that the strong smell of his pipe tobacco would mask his liquor-laden breath wafting across the fire. Wolves and coyotes could come in close to worry the horses. He handed Zeke a big-faced, brass-ringed pocket timepiece. 'Give me a shake in a coupla hours for me to do my stint, OK?'

Houseman watched his deputy walk back to the creek with Bear Paw's coffee and knew that he had got everything wrong about his new deputy. His downgrading of the boy had been the bad-minded thoughts of a catankerous old bastard. He could find no fault with Deputy Ezekiel Isaiah Butler. If the truth be known, the boy deserved a better partner than him, a man his deputy could look up to. He lusted for the flesh of a female outside wedlock, and was a regular drinker of corn liquor. An out-and-out sinner in the boy's eyes. Though he didn't consider the killing of owlhoots in the line of duty sinful in any way. Houseman gave a slack-mouthed whiskey-induced grin. As his deputy had stated he was only carrying out the Good Lord's work, fighting the good fight, sending bad-asses to Hell where they belonged. Warm inside with the whiskey and warm thoughts of the widow Hedgepath, Houseman soon dropped off into a deep sleep.

Clyde Packard, a small, rat-faced man, belly-crawled back to Ed Newton, also hugging dirt on the edge of the creek. 'There's only two of them, Ed,' he said softly. 'One at the horses, the other stretched out at the fire. 'Easy pickin's, Ed.'

'But there's three horses, Clyde,' replied Ed. Ed was a big, heavy-paunched, grey-whiskered individual though as mean-faced looking as his partner.

'One of them could be a pack animal,' Clyde said.

Ed, the cautious one, took another look into the darkness about him. 'OK,' he said. 'But we take them alive. We need all the gear there is in that camp. Horses, guns and their clothes, the whole caboodle. We're been eatin' grass too long; we're entitled to thick steaks, fine whiskey and the company of purty lookin' females.' Ed cold-smiled. 'Bullet-holed and blood-stained clothes don't make good trade goods.' Ed gave a gap-toothed smirk. 'I'll go and say howdee to the fella with the horses; you do likewise with his pard at the fire.'

Clyde was feeling good as he crawled towards the horse line. Ed was right, they were long past due to strike it lucky. Penny-ante robberies only raked them in a few days' eating money.

Josh, smelling a stranger to the camp close by, gave out a loud snort and kicked out with its back legs. Before a half-dozing Zeke caught on that the marshal's horse was sending him a danger signal he felt his head being jerked back then the coldness of a knife blade pressing against his exposed throat. 'If you try to holler, pilgrim,' Clyde hissed, 'You'll get well and truly dead.' He reached down and took Zeke's pistol. Zeke froze, partly with fear, but mostly with tear, moist-eyed anger at being caught off guard, letting down Marshal Houseman.

Marshal Houseman had let himself down. He had been dreaming about the widow Hedgepath and the next thing he knew he had been hauled up off the ground and was eyeballing a big, hairy-faced man waving a knife under his nose. The good feelings raised by the widow and the whiskey vanished.

'We've come here to rob you, mister,' Ed said conversationally. 'But it will cause us no sweat if you force us to kill you.'

Ed pricked Houseman's neck with the knife point, drawing a thin trickle of blood.

Houseman winced, and cursed silently but offered

no resistance. The bear of a man who held the knife had all the edge. He prayed that his deputy hadn't acted wildly.

The big man dragged him on to his feet then Houseman heard him call out, 'Bring the other fella in, Clyde!'

A much relieved Houseman saw that Zeke, though down in the mouth looking, seemed unharmed, was being escorted to the fire by a smaller man than the owlhoot holding him. But the knife he was fisting was every bit as big as the one digging into his back. He gave his deputy a quick, hard-eyed glance warning him to let things they had no control of to run their course. Their getting-even time would come later, of that he was certain.

'I told you that it would be easy pickin's, Ed,' a grinning Clyde said.

Ed jabbed Houseman in the ribs with the knife, signing his own death warrant Houseman thought grimly. 'Where's the owner of the third horse?' he asked.

'There's only two of us,' Houseman replied. 'One of the horses is a pack animal; you can see that there's only two saddles here. Me and the boy are traders. We're headin' for the Strip to buy some of those fancy worked blankets the Injun squaws make.'

He hoped to hell that Bear Paw would stay put in the cave. The robbing sons-of-bitches were riding at full-cock and seeing another man coming in, after lying to his back teeth that it was only a two-man camp, would set off a small massacre, him, the kid and Bear Paw being the victims.

Bear Paw, draped in the blanket, came slowly alive

once more as the heat from the fire and the stomach-warming coffee began to spread through his chilled body. The icy-cold water of the creek had stung his flesh as though he was lashing himself with strands of barbed fence wire, numbing him to the bone and making it difficult for him to breathe. If the boy had not brought the blanket and helped him make it to the cave and lit the fire he would have died, clean and sober, in the creek.

The fire began to smoke and Bear Paw stepped out of the cave to get some fresh air. He glanced idly across the creek, the camp had visitors; he could see the silhouettes of four men standing at the fire. He heard the snorting and hoof shuffling of horses close by on his side of the creek. Curious, he walked in the direction of the sounds and came on to two tethered horses, rifles still in their boots. That set Bear Paw wondering some more. Why hadn't the marshal's night visitors rode openly into the camp? He was rapidly getting the feeling that the others' business at the camp wasn't just to pass the time of the day and share their fire and coffee with men they had met up with on the trail.

Convinced that he had read the situation right, Bear Paw pulled out one of the rifles and, shrugging off the blanket, waded silently across the creek, risking the death of a thousand cuts again.

He crept close enough to the camp to see that his gut feelings hadn't played him wrong. Marshal Houseman and his young deputy lay stretched out face down on the ground with the two strangers standing over them with pistols in their hands.

Bear Paw did some rapid thinking knowing that he

had to make his play to rescue the two lawmen fast before he froze to death. He couldn't gun down the two raiders, even at this short range for a rifle, the way the gun was shaking in his hands.

Now armed with a pistol, and the two traders kissing the dirt, Ed relaxed somewhat, enough to give a twist of a grin of triumph. Him and Clyde had sure got the jump on the old fart and the kid.

'Clyde,' he said. 'Go and get our horses then pick up the other three on the way back and bring them into the camp then we can start collectin' what we paid a call on these, gents for. I'll make sure that they keep huggin' the ground.'

An equally happy-looking Clyde made his way to the creek doing some rough calculating on how much cash him and Ed would rake in selling the traders' gear. He was still smiling when Bear Paw killed him.

Bear Paw had only meant to knock out the small raider. Holding the rifle by the barrel he had used it as a club but having practically lost all feeling in his arms with the cold he had swung the rifle too hard, smashing in the back of Clyde's skull in a mess of splintered bone and blood, killing him dead before he crumpled to the ground. Bear Paw muttered some Indian curses. The first time sober for years and he had killed a white man. Even if the white man was a thief it was still a hanging matter for an Indian. Trying to forget his possible short-lived future, Bear Paw put the second part of his rescue plan in motion.

Ed gave an involuntary jerk of alarm as the shrill, bubbling shriek of an Indian 'death hulloe' rang out over the camp. He lost his smile and good feelings. Taking his attention, and gun, from his prisoners he gazed fearfully into the dark belt of brush and timber that bordered the creek.

'You didn't give me time to tell you, mister,' Houseman said, hiding his grin, knowing that Bear Paw had sobered up enough to work out the situation in the camp. 'That me and the boy cut the sign of a sizeable band of hostiles before we made camp. I figure that your pard must have just met up with them.'

A dirty-mouthing, scared-to-hell Ed glared down at Houseman. The marshal rubbed in the fear the big man was feeling to keep him worried and jump-nerved until Bear Paw made his play.

'I don't know what you were goin' to do to me and the boy after you had robbed us, mister, but it looks as though we're all goin' to end up the same way now, dead. And it ain't goin' to be a pleasant dyin'.'

Ed, fear clawing sickeningly in the pit of his stomach, did some more cursing. He felt like breaking into tears at the sudden and dramatic change in his and Clyde's fortunes. Somewhere skulking in the brush was a bunch of bare-assed red devils who had put paid to his pard, lifted his hair no doubt, and were about to come storming in on him.

While Ed was doing his fretting, and cursing, Houseman inched closer to where his gunbelt lay, so that he could back up Bear Paw's play when it came. At least, he thought optimistically, it would be a one-to-one confrontation; Bear Paw must have put paid the the small rat-faced thief.

When Bear Paw made his move it caused captives

and captor to have sudden nerve twitching limbs. A wide-eyed, slack-jawed Ed caught sight of a bloodthirsty howling jaybird naked Indian leaping at him from out of the darkness. The frightening spectacle froze his reactions for a few vital seconds, long enough for Bear Paw to clear the ground to the fire and hit him with a sweeping blow with the rifle before he could pull off a shot from his pistol. Ed dropped to the ground straight and true like a felled tree.

The rifle slipped out of Bear Paw's hands and he folded in the middle, drawing in deep rasping breaths. He shivered with cold and the reaction of his wild charge and the killing, maybe, of two white men. Houseman and Zeke sprang to their feet and walked over to him, Houseman picking up his long-tailed. plains coat and draping it across Bear Paw's shoulders.

'You did OK, Bear Paw,' Houseman said. 'The sonsuvbitches caught me and the boy off guard. They were intent on takin' everything in the camp but our drawers.' He grinned. 'You fire-ballin' in frightened the crap out of the three of us.' Face hardening again he said, 'I take it that this fella's pard ain't no longer a threat to us?'

Bear Paw straightened up. 'I've killed him, Marshal,' Bear Paw replied. 'Hit him too hard. So you'll have to take me to Fort Smith to stand trial for murder.'

Houseman laughed. 'Stand trial for murder?' Why, old Parker will give you a medal for savin' the lives of two of his marshals.'

'Would those two thieves have killed us, Marshalf?' Zeke asked.

'They would have had to if they found the marshals'

badges in our pockets, Deputy.' Houseman looked at Bear Paw. 'We unpinned them before crossin' over into the Strip on account we're doin' some snoopin' there for Judge Parker and Fort Smith lawmen ain't officially allowed in the Strip. Goin' back to your question, Deputy, if those two sonsuvbitches knew they were robbin' two US marshals, and the hell that would raise for them, to save their dirty hides they would have to kill us. So you ain't goin' to make that trip to Fort Smith, Bear Paw.'

They heard a groaning and moaning behind them and, on swinging round, saw that the big raider was coming to.

'Well, you ain't killed this fella, Bear Paw,' Houseman said, as he kicked Ed's gun to the other side of the fire.

Slowly, with hammers thumping away in his head, Ed struggled on to his feet, standing swaying there with dizziness and pain. He focused a bleary-eyed gaze on his three captors, the bare-ass naked Indian, now partly covered by a coat, the old man and the kid. The old bastard was favouring him with a bad-eyed look, up setting him further.

'Mister,' Houseman grated, 'you and your weasel of a pard made one big mistake raidin' a US marshal and his deputy's camp.'

Judge Parker's marshals! Ed flinched as though he had been struck by a heavy fist and dolefully wondered how bad could a man's luck get. Him and Clyde should have stuck to robbing stores and rolling drunks in side alleys.

'Though you're luckier than your pard,' Houseman

61

continued. 'He's lyin' back there dead. Bein' that me and my deputy have urgent business elsewhere I ain't got the time to take you back to Fort Smith to decorate Judge Parker's grand scaffold. I'm lettin' you go on your way, after you've seen to it that your late pard is decently covered up. You stay here at the fire, Bear Paw, keep yourself warm; Deputy Butler will go to the cave for your clothes.' He dug Ed in the ribs with his pistol. 'OK, let's go before I change my mind about not haulin' you back to Arkansas for causin' me to lose a night's sleep.'

Ed walked unsteadily towards the creek helped along by regular sharp jabs from Houseman's pistol. Having narrowly escaping being clubbed to death and how near he had been to be heading for Fort Smith and a hanging, Ed kept his murderous thoughts regarding the son-of-a-bitch lawman from showing on his face.

After he had covered his dead partner's body with rocks, Houseman allowed Ed to ride away from the camp, minus his guns and belt of reloads. Now the three of them were sitting at the fire, none of them feeling like sleep. Zeke and a fully dressed Bear Paw were talking softly to each other, Houseman, craving a pull at the whiskey bottle, keeping his own counsel as he tried to figure out how he could, as Judge Parker had suggested, sneak across into the Strip and do some snooping around to discover the whereabouts of the raiders. As well as the sheriff of Bitter Water Springs knowing him as a marshal, there must be dozens of lawbreakers in the territory with whom he had exchanged lead to avoid capture. There was no way, Houseman finally thought, that he could do any sneaking around in the Strip without being fingered as a lawman.

He looked across the fire at his deputy and Bear Paw, still chatting, and a slow smile crept across his face. Even the most leery-eyed of owlhooters wouldn't tag the boy as a marshal; he ought to be able to show his face openly in Bitter Water Springs and ask some discreet questions about Stacey, the hiring man Belle Starr had mentioned, and keep his eyes open for any bunches of hard men who raised his suspicions. Bear Paw, now he seemed to have quit downing fire water, could quiz his own people for information about the night riders. They would be more open with one of their own than a white-eye.

Houseman's smile stretched to a wide open grin. In making his enquiries Deputy Marshal Ezekiel Isaiah Butler would have to pay a visit to saloons, maybe bawdy houses, dens of iniquity in his eyes. The boy would get his bellyful of the wicked ways of the citizens of the Strip, though Houseman opined that his deputy's religious fervour would not allow him to be corrupted. He knew it was no great shakes of a plan but he couldn't come up with a better one.

He would keep low until the pair got lucky and got a clear lead as to where the gang holed-up when they were not burning out Indian farmers. Then Houseman thought would come the hard bit. He scowled. It was OK Judge Parker saying that he had only to locate the gang's hole-up then he would have a whole posse of marshals riding out of Fort Smith to do the rounding up. Houseman's scowl deepened. If they did get lucky and found out where the gang was they would have to be rounded up there and then, or the sons-of-bitches could go off on a raid then lie low some place else. And how could he and the boy surround a bunch of desperadoes? He didn't know who was the most loco, the judge for sending him, or him for taking on the job.

His scheme depended on Bear Paw acting as an unpaid deputy marshal, and didn't take up with his drinking habits again. Houseman gave a twitch of a grin. He would have to ask the boy to do a little preaching to Bear Paw warning him of his 'sinning' downing the 'demon' drink. The extra guns and reloads would allow him to arm up Bear Paw if he wanted to go the whole hog of being a marshal. The spare horse he would leave with the Paxtons while they did their scouting around.

Then Houseman put his mind to thinking just who the raiders were. Were they a bunch of Indian haters? Their hatred for their red brethren strong enough to want to drive them off their legally held land? He'd heard talk back there in Fort Smith that the Cherokee Strip was about to be opened up to a whole army of sodbusters seeking a piece of growing land. So the raiding could be organized by someone indulging in the old frontier way of acquiring property by forcing off the legitimate owners. It would have to be someone with a big bankroll to pay the men who were doing the dirty work, Houseman concluded. He grunted. What the hell did it matter why the sons-of-bitches were doing the raiding, all he was being paid to do was to seek them out.

He would put his plan to Zeke and Bear Paw when they broke up camp in the morning, right now Houseman reckoned he had done enough brain work for the night and closed his eyes to try and get a couple of hours or so sleep before dawn. He smiled. He didn't think that the camp would be raided again, not when he had the red hellion, Bear Paw on watch.

EIGHT

A foul-tempered Calvin T. Striker glared balefully out of the hotel window on to the street below and the townsfolk going about their daily business – loud-mouthed, horse-faced men and their equally, drab-garbed, horse-faced womenfolk, and the overpowering stink of cow-shit tinged dust drifting through the open window,

He was eyeballing Main Street, Bitter Water Springs. Striker gave a derisive snort. Main Street: was no better than a broad farm track. And as for the hotel, the best in town Frazer had assured him when he had picked him up at the stage depot, why, he wouldn't stable his string of Arabian mares in the place. And he had to spend the night in the barn of a building as the east-bound stage did not leave until noon tomorrow.

He'd had a bath, of sorts, in a wooden tub in a draughty outhouse, filled by buckets of tepid water brought in by an old Indian with a face so frightening he dared not complain about the water not being too hot. He could still taste the dust from the ball-aching stage ride from the rail depot. Not wanting to stay any longer than was necessary in this hellhole of a place he had asked Frazer to accompany him to his room to appraise him of the situation that had brought him here as soon as Frazer had drawn up the buggy outside the hotel. Still standing, and not offering Frazer a seat, Striker gave his agent a curt nod to begin stating the problem holding back the growth of the Indian Territory Land Development Company.

'The man I hired, Mr Striker,' Frazer began, 'had five of his men killed on their last raid and he has notified me that if I want the raiding to continue he'll have to hire more men, and at a much higher price. Even the type of cutthroat he hires values his dirty hide.'

Striker hard-eyed Frazer. Of course he wanted the raiding to continue. He had sunk almost every blasted cent he had to get his hands on as much good farming land as he could before the deadline, now he was risking someone else's money. The raiding had to go on, but not at an unlimited cost. He broke his stone-faced, silence.

'The company has had some extra funding invested in it, Frazer. So it can afford to meet the higher hiring fee this fella—'

'Stacey, Mr Striker, Wes Stacey,' interrupted Frazer.

'Yeah, well, whoever,' Striker continued. 'So he can start up his raiding again, at once!' Again his chilly-eyed gaze swept over Frazer. 'Demands within reason, Mr Frazer, understand? You know who you are dealing with so if you feel that this Wes Stacey is trying to milk you, find someone else to do the task. I'll place money in the town's bank for you to draw on before I leave. I and the board are relying on you, Frazer, to clear up this little difficulty.' Striker's smile was as icy as his looks had been. 'Or I may be looking for a new agent.'

Frazer left the hotel as sour-gutted as Calvin T. Striker, cursing himself for acting as an agent for Striker's illegal business activities lawbreaking activities that could see him in jail, or shot by irate Indian homesteaders. It was all right for the high and mighty Mr Striker to come West for a few hours to lay down the law to him, the son-of-a-bitch couldn't get his fat ass back fast enough to Chicago and all the home comforts and luxuries of a big Eastern city.

He hadn't to live in a dog dirt town and negotiate with killers like Stacey. Stacey was a short-fused character and he'd had the frightening thought that the fuse was about to blow when Stacey told him of the shooting down of over half his gang. If he had made any critical comment about the handling of the ballsed-up raid Stacey would have pulled out the big pistol, sheathed on his right hip, and shot him dead where he stood.

Frazer headed for the Long Branch saloon where the gunman would be drinking at the bar. He would give him a knowing nod to indicate that he would meet him at their usual rendezvous in the morning. His demand for extra payment to raise another gang being granted ought to put Stacey in a less stressful mood. Frazer would willing debate with any other lawyer the financial pros and cons of a piece of real estate and what it was worth in hard cash, but in spite of Striker's warning he wasn't about to risk his life arguing with a professional killer over the going rate for a bunch of fire raisers. What figure Stacey asked for he would honour it.

NINE

'Haul up here, boys,' Houseman said, bringing his horse to a halt on a ridge overlooking a shack and several outbuildings. 'If we've followed Sheriff Parsons' directions right we oughta be gazin' down on Mr Paxton's place. But we'll stay put up here until we make ourselves known and the sodbuster invites us to come on down. It ain't healthy for three strangers, one of them an Injun, to ride in uninvited like on a family that's shot five bad-assed raiders.'

'Hello the house!' he called out. 'I'm Marshal Houseman from Fort Smith, Judge Parker asked me to pay a call on you! These are my two deputies!'

Which was true to a point as far as Bear Paw was concerned. As they crossed over into the Strip Houseman had told Bear Paw that he was free to go his own way, though he would be grateful if he would ride along with him and his deputy for a few more days.

'You'd be a help in our search for those raiders I told you about, Bear Paw,' he said. 'Your people are more likely to answer your questions about the raiders than a white-eye lawman. More so when it's white men who are doin' the raidin'.' He grinned. 'I can't pay you, but I'll see that you don't starve. And I'll swear you in as a special deputy which will give you the legal right to shoot down any man white, red or brown who draws his gun on any of us. You ain't beholden to me any, Bear Paw, for you to take up my request. It's me and Deputy Butler who are beholden to you for gettin' us outa that hairy situation back at the camp.'

'We're all even, Marshal Houseman,' replied Bear Paw. 'You and Deputy Butler saved my life when you escorted me out of Bitter Water Springs.' He grinned. 'And helped me to live without a whiskey bottle in my hand. I've never seen the kinfolk I have here for years, a few more days' absence won't make any difference. Swear me in, Marshal.'

Houseman had mumbled the swearing in phrases as Bear Paw raised his right hand then he ordered Zeke to hand over one of the spare pistols and gunbelts to the new deputy.

'There's someone coming out of the shack, Marshal,' Zeke said.

Houseman saw a man step out on to the porch, holding a rifle. Then a boy, also carrying a rifle, appeared from round the far corner of the shack. Houseman gave out a 'Well I'll be damned!' as a young girl joined her pa on the porch cradling a shotgun in her arms with a barrel as long as she was tall.

Houseman smiled. 'Ma ain't behind those drapes drawing a bead on us with a Sharps' buffalo gun, is she?' he yelled.

'You and your deputies can come on down, Marshal!' Adam Paxton shouted. 'And you and your men are more than welcome to share the food Ma's got ready. As soon as she's put aside the Gatling gun!'

The three lawmen allowed their horses to pick their own way down the grade, but before they reached the flat Bear Paw said, 'I'll see to the horses, Marshal, it isn't likely that Mr Paxton will welcome an Indian sitting down at his table.'

Houseman swung round in his saddle and gave his new deputy a steely-eyed glare. 'You're a duly sworn in deputy marshal, mister, just the same as me and Deputy Butler. If that don't sit well with yon sodbuster then we'll have to eat what Deputy Butler can rustle up, OK?'

Deputy Butler gave a low agreeing grunt. He had never expected an old sinner like Marshal Houseman to believe in the brotherhood of man.

They dismounted in front of the shack and Paxton stepped down from the porch to greet them. Houseman introduced himself and his Indian scout, Bear Paw, to Paxton.

Adam Paxton gave Bear Paw a welcoming nod. Judge Parker had taken his complaint serious enough to send an Indian scout to the Strip.

'That's my boy, David, and daughter, Sarah Jane,' he said jerking his chin over his shoulder to the pair of youngsters standing on the porch.

Houseman noticed that David Paxton had the same direct-eyed look as his pa had. A boy, he reckoned, Paxton would be proud of. And by what he had been told, he had proved his worth in the shoot-out with the raiders. The girl, the confident way she was holding the shotgun, must have also played her part. He glanced at

Deputy Butler and his lips twitched in a slight smile. His deputy was goggle-eying the girl. Not that he didn't blame him. She was a long corn-coloured haired beauty who would stir the blood of any city boy.

'Unsaddle the horses, Deputy!' he said sharply, to bring him out of his trance. 'And if Mr Paxton will tell us where his watering trough is you can water them.'

'Yeah, yeah, sure, Marshal,' replied Zeke, his face reddening. The way he had been staring at the girl must have made her as embarrassed as he was. Why he had done so had him puzzled. He had never before met a girl he couldn't take his gaze off. Then she sweet-smiled at him and he heard her say, 'I'll take him to the tank.' A statement which further unsettled Zeke.

Sarah Jane was also wondering why she had been so outspoken. Deputy Butler wasn't exactly the handsome, smart-suited beau whom she had fantacized would come riding in one day and sweep her off her feet and take her East to some big city. By his ill-fitting hand-me-down clothes, Sarah Jane guessed that Deputy Butler, before he wore a marshal's badge, had been a backwoods boy. She gave an inner grin. And by the way he was gawping at her he hadn't had much to do with girls.

Yet Deputy Butler's look hadn't made her feel uneasy and angry as the gazes cast at her by the young males in Bitter Water Springs when accompanying her pa, or Dave, on the regular wagon trips to town for supplies. For some unexplained reason his look gave her a warm, pleasant feeling. Resting the shotgun up against the wall of the cabin she stepped down and took hold of the reins of two of the horses.

She smiled again and said, 'The water tank is this way, Deputy Butler.' Then she led the horses off towards the barn.

A burning-cheeked, tongued-tied Deputy Butler followed in her trail leading the other two mounts.

Houseman grinned at Paxton. 'That purty daughter of yours has sure got my deputy's attention. I reckon it must be a worry to you raisin' a fine-lookin' girl in a territory roamin' with lawless, hot-blooded men. But she'll come to no harm with Deputy Butler; he's mighty religious. I hear him sayin' his prayers every night as he lays down his blanket. Though that don't prevent him for bein' a first-class deputy marshal.'

'A mite more dedicated marshals in the territory wouldn't come amiss,' Paxton said.

'Amen to that,' replied Houseman. 'It would make my life a damn sight easier.' He grinned at Paxton. 'I figure you're wondering why we've an extra horse with us. We sorta picked it up after a little trouble we had at our last night camp. Trouble Deputy Bear Paw put right for us.'

Paxton, seeing Deputy Bear Paw's face harden, didn't need to ask what sort of trouble it had been.

'Now, tell me about your trouble, Mr Paxton,' Houseman said. 'I heard you made the raiders pay dearly for their night visit here.'

'I don't know why the bunch rode in to burn me out, Marshal,' Paxton replied. 'Or who the hell they were. Even Sheriff Blakemore couldn't place any of the men we killed. But the bastard who was runnin' them must have got himself another gang of barn burners because a Cherokee farm only a few miles west of here was raided last night.'

Houseman's face became as Indian looking as Bear Paw's. Cold-voiced, he said, 'I'd be obliged, Deputy, if you'd go and get our long guns and tell Deputy Butler to speed up waterin' the horses and bring them back here. We could have to do some fast movin' around.'

'There's no need for the alert, Marshal,' Paxton said. 'The sonsuvbitches do their burnin' at night.'

Houseman swung round and faced Paxton and his son. Still icy-voiced he said, 'I ain't bein' a blowhard when I say that I've had dealin's with night riders, road agents, cattle-lifters, and other suchlike owlhoots for more years than I can remember. One thing I've learnt, not without the pain of havin' several lumps of lead shot into my hide, is that you never drop your guard, day or night, when a bunch of law-breakin' scum are doin' their damnedest close by you. You and your kin gave the fella who's bossin' the gang a bloody setback, caused him to lose face in front of his wild boys. Any man likes to be seen to walk tall, especially a hard man bossin' over a bunch of likewise no-good sonsuvbitclies.'

Paxton's face took on a pinched-assed look. Worriedly he said, 'I'd better set up a lookout post on the ridge. I'll get—'

'I'll stand the first watch, Mr Paxton,' Bear Paw interrupted, having returned from the barn. 'If that's OK with you, Marshal?' he added, as he handed Houseman his rifle.

Houseman saw the pleading look in Bear Paw's eyes willing him to allow him to stand the watch. He reckoned that Bear Paw, as well as garbed in clothes that should have been burnt, was still suffering the swamp fever-like shakes of a newly reformed drunk and wouldn't be at his ease sitting down at a white family's eating table.

'OK, Deputy,' he said. 'You do that. Any sightin' of fast-moving' trail dust headin' this way, sound the alarm.'

'I'll see that you don't go hungry, Mr Bear Paw,' Paxton said. 'My boy will bring you some chow as soon as Ma dishes it out. And that won't be long, Marshal, so I reckon we should go indoors; because Ma don't like her cookin' to get cold. You go, Dave, and tell your sister and Deputy Butler that it's chow time.'

Houseman placed his rifle at the side of the door before he entered the shack. Though he didn't show it he wasn't very happy about the way things were shaping up.

His plan had been to show up at the farm to prove to Paxton that Judge Parker had responded favourably to his plea for help then let his deputies do their snooping around the territory for a couple of days or so. He didn't expect them to pick up any leads on the whereabouts of the raiders, but again it would show Paxton that Judge Parker's marshals were doing their best to track down the night riders. Then he and Deputy Butler would hightail it back into his section of the Nations and pick up the tumbleweed wagon and start earning their pay by hauling wanted men back to Fort Smith and Judge Parker's court house.

The news of the raiding starting up again was causing Houseman to rethink his plans. He had never expected any more raiding from the gang, or what was left of it, after riding off with five of their buddies lying dead just outside this shack. But they had. And that got Houseman pondering about who the man was who was paying them, and why?

One thing was for sure: he couldn't leave the Paxton family on their own to beat off another raid, which he had told the sodbuster would more than likely take place. If he and his deputies rode out and left them to fend for themselves and the worst happened, Judge Parker would have *him* dangling on one of his gallows. And, damn it, he would deserve to swing there.

Mrs Paxton, a plumpish, comely-looking woman, greeted him with a welcoming smile and Houseman put his worries at the back of his mind until he'd had his fill of the steaming dishes of food she was laying on the table. After years of trail fare, part warmed beans, greasy sow belly and coffee that tasted like tar, the mouth-watering smell of the home-cooked food was giving him a craving to start eating as strong as Bear Paw must have had for the whiskey.

The three marshals had dined well and were mounted up ready to ride out on the trail of the raiders, Houseman having come up with a new plan which was an extension of his original one. He would quarter the territory within a three- or four-mile circuit of the farm acting as a sort of one man picket guard for the Paxtons, hoping that if he did spot the raiders he would have time to ass-kick it back to the farm to warn them that trouble was heading their way. If he hadn't raised any alarm by dusk he would return to the farm and stand the dangerous night watch with them.

Deputy Butler and Bear Paw would be carrying out what he'd discussed with them. Thankfully the pair of them had both accepted to carry out his makeshift plan without any disagreement.

Houseman called a halt where the Bitter Water Springs trail cut away from the Kansas turnpike. 'We go our own ways now, Deputies,' he said. 'I'll expect both of you back at the Paxtons' three days from now, sooner if you pick up some good leads, OK?' He gave Zeke a closed-eyed look. In spite of acknowledging that the boy had the making of a first-class lawman Houseman had the uncomfortable feeling that he was sending a Daniel into a lion's den. The questioning he was asking him to do could get him killed. He partly consoled himself with the thought that the boy had chosen to be a marshal so he had to accept the dangers that came with the badge.

'Don't push yourself too hard in Bitter Water Springs, Deputy,' he warned. 'Along with this fella Stacey and his gang we're seekin', there's other hard men, men wanted by the law who will gun you down even if they only suspect you of bein' a peace officer. And there'll be other no-good characters, dark side-alley thieves who'll gladly pistol whip you, or knife you for what you're wearin', or what they hope you've got in your pockets.' Houseman didn't mention the cat-house whores who, with their sweet-talking ways would easily make a country hick part with everything he possessed, thinking he was on his way to paradise. His gaze became flintier. 'And no tryin' to lead back on to the paths of righteousness any of those sinful folk you're goin' among. You're actin' as my scout in Bitter

Water Springs and good scouts don't draw attention to themselves, OK?'

'OK, Marshal,' a sombre-faced Zeke replied.

Houseman watched them ride out before he began his own scouting. He saw them exchange farewell salutes as Bear Paw drew away, heading south to the latest target of the raiders. Frustrated at knowing he was out of control of any awkward situation the pair might raise up he vented his anger with another bout of cursing on the head of the 'hanging' judge.

Zeke rode with mixed feelings of apprehension and excitement at Marshal Houseman having enough faith in him to allow him to operate on his own. Zeke wasn't underrating the dangers he could meet up with, the marshal had made sure of that, but he believed with God's guidance he would help to put paid to the night riders and end the fears of Sarah Jane and her family.

Thinking of the sweet-smiling Sarah Jane made him forget his worries for a while. He would have liked to have had a longer chat with her as they watered the horses but Bear Paw's alerting had put a sudden end to his pleasant hopes. Zeke's lips hardened in thin determined lines. By golly, he thought resolutely, he would not let the faith Marshal Houseman had in him come to nought even if meant that he had to break the sixth Commandment.

Stacey ordered himself another congratulatory shot of whiskey before he left the Long Branch and made his way across the street to spend an hour or so bouncing Sophia, the cat-house's latest girl, a blonde hailing from Minnesota.

The first raid with his new gang, six strong, four of them blood-mixed border cutthroats, had gone smoothly, though Stacey knew he could only rely on their loyalty as long as he dished out the cash after the raid. They had stormed in and out of the farm leaving behind them the flames of the burning shack and barns lighting up the night sky without a shot being fired back at them.

Soon, he thought, it would be time to settle up with the sodbuster who had downed his boys. He cold-grinned. The shyster would be paying for the raid, but that was one burning out he would do for free. He downed his whiskey to leave his hired guns to spend their due drinking and playing cards and fooling around with the two-dollar a session saloon girls and walked out of the saloon to end his good-feeling day with one hell of a good-feeling night.

TEN

Zeke rode into Bitter Water Springs bracing himself for his first visit to the town's saloons, or dens of iniquity as his pa named them, to carry out Marshal Houseman's orders. In those dens there would be bunches of men, local citizens, crews from the nearby ranches, spending their hard-earned dues on the devil's brew and the turn of a card. And wary-eyed visaged, armed-to-the-teeth men, who could be members of the gang of night raiders. How he was going to find out for sure if he had spotted any suspicious like characters had him puzzled.

All he could do, Zeke reasoned, if he picked out a likely bunch would be to ride back to the Paxton farm and tell the marshal of his suspicions and leave it to the experienced lawman to plan the next move. Or maybe he could trail the men after they had finished their drinking back to where they had made their camp then belly crawl close enough to hear any talk about another raid taking place then maybe get the drop on them. Zeke gave a broad grin. And just as far-fetched someday he would be Saint Zeke. Though anything was worth trying if it prevented another raid on the Paxton farm.

Bitter Water Springs wasn't as big or busy looking as Fort Smith and as he let his mount have its head going along Main Street Zeke was pleased to note that the town boasted only one saloon. He suddenly caught sight of some girls standing on the balcony of a double-storeyed building next to the saloon garbed only in short shifts. Fallen doves unashamedly showing off their near naked bodies in public. One of the girls shouted, 'Are you going to pay a call on us, country boy?'

Zeke shrank in his saddle, too embarrassed to lift his head and look at the now loudly giggling girls. He forced his horse into a near gallop to get out of range of their catcalling, hoping that he was riding in the right direction for the livery barn.

When Zeke came back along Main Street after seeing his horse stabled he kept close to the store fronts on the same side as the whorehouse. He made it to the porch of the saloon without more ribbing from the fallen doves. He pushed open the swing doors and entered Satan's domain.

Zeke noticed that there were many hands carrying out the Devil's work, several barkeeps serving strong liquor, men dealing cards, throwing dice on the gambling tables and heavily painted girls wearing short, gaudy, spangled dresses brazenly sitting on some of the customers' knees partaking of the demon drink. Laughing loudly as though there was no shame in either of their actions. Zeke had never seen so much sin going on in one place before; it almost overwhelmed him making him wonder if he had the moral strength to go ahead with the task Marshal Houseman had given him.

Saying a short silent prayer he weaved his way through the drinkers to reach the bar. He found a space just vacated by a man who was being led up the stairs at the right of the bar by a widely grinning saloon girl. Once settled there he turned and faced the saloon's customers and tried to figure out which of the several bunches of men drinking or playing cards together, had the cut of men who earned the money they were spending by raiding farms.

A snarled, 'What you drinkin', bub!' stopped Zeke's eyeballing and he swung round to face a sweating, sour-faced barkeep. 'Make your goddamned mind up, I ain't got all night to wait on your pleasure! It's pay day for the ranch hands and the sonsuvbitches are thirsty.'

'Whiskey, please,' replied Zeke. A soda pop would have suited him but the marshal had told him that 'scouts' didn't draw unnecessary attention to themselves. Asking for a soda pop in a crowded saloon would have him the talk of the town, let alone the butt of every drinker in the saloon. After paying for the glass of whiskey the heavy-handed barkeep thumped down in front of him, Zeke closed-eyed the amber-coloured liquor for a moment or two then, to fit in with the rest of the drinkers, he picked up the glass and took a tentative sip at it. He gasped as the fiery liquor clawed at his throat and brought tears to his eyes.

He knew now why his pa named it the 'devil's brew' and the Indians called it 'fire water'. Zeke couldn't understand why Bear Paw had such a craving need for the soul and body-destroying poison. Reckoning that he had done all the drinking he was going to do, ever, he half turned from the bar and began carrying out his mission, that of trying to spot any suspected night raiders among the bunches of drinkers and card players at the tables in front of him. And found out he had given himself a hard task. Every other customer in the saloon had the look of a man wanted by the law. Though Zeke knew that didn't make him a night raider.

His searching gaze fell on five men playing cards at a table to his left. Four of them were swarthy, hard-planed-faced men and Zeke catalogued them as 'breeds. The fifth player, though a white man, had the same stone-faced visage as his partners. They were playing cards together yet there was no good-humoured joshing and bantering going on between them as was taking place at the other tables so he didn't think that they were a ranch crew, or a bunch of local citizens enjoying a night out. He had seen suchlike characters roped up on their horses, or squatting chained up in a tumbleweed wagon, being escorted into Fort Smith by US marshals to face retribution from Judge Parker for their sinful lawless ways.

Zeke thought it would be worth his while trailing them when they left the saloon to find out if they were a ranch crew. If they bedded down for the night in the open then it was riding back to Marshal Houseman time.

Cursing his bad luck, Clegg threw his cards down on the table. Jaundiced-eyed he watched the grinning Silvero scoop up the poker pot, most of it his money, the easy-come-by money he had been paid for burning out Indian farmers. He had a gut feeling that the Mex 'breed had been dealing off the bottom of the deck but if he called him a no-good card sharp to his face he would have to back his accusation with his gun. Clegg figured that he was fast enough to put Silvero down, though not fast enough to take on the guns of his three *compadres* having no doubt that the 'breeds would back one of their own kind, even if he was a cheating son-of-a-bitch, against a gringo.

Clegg's face twisted into a scowl as he swung round in his chair and met the stare of the kid standing at the bar. His scowl turned into a full-blooded wolf-like snarl. He was spoiling for a fight, fist, boot, knife or gun, to vent his anger at his losses. He thin-smiled. The young hayseed at the bar would do just dandy. He had the soft-faced look of a kid who wore his belted pistol just to impress the saloon girls. He pushed back his chair and got to his feet and faced the hayseed Zeke.

'Why the hell are you gawpin' at me, kid'? his roar cut above the general hubbub of the saloon. 'You put me off my game!'

The drinkers at the bar sidled away hurriedy from Zeke, leaving him standing there on his own as though he was a carrier of the spotted plague. Clegg's menacing presence had also cleared a path to the bar.

A fleeting chill of fear swept over Zeke as he stared back at the savage-faced gunman in the now silent saloon. Were the 'breeds at the table really the night riders, he wondered? Had he somehow unwittingly blown his cover and they knew he was a lawman? If so, why had the big man accused him of spoiling his game? Or was he only saying that so he could have an excuse for shooting him? Whatever reason didn't matter. The gunman was forcing him to draw his pistol or be branded as a coward. Then he would have to hand in his US marshal's badge. As quickly as it had come his scared feeling vanished. He bold-eyed his threat.

'If you reckon that I've caused you any upset,' he said, hard-voiced, 'then you have my apologies. I came into this saloon to have a drink, not to cause any trouble. If you're not prepared to accept my word on that then you're goin' to get the trouble you seem to be seeking. I'll have to gun you down.'

Clegg rocked back on his heels. 'Gun me down?' his voice was a bull-like roar. 'A ragged-assed ploughboy gunnin' me down! Like hell you will!' Dirty-mouthing him he scrabbled for his pistol. His haste proved his undoing. He brought his gun into play first, but still unsteady with anger at being talked down by a kid, his shot passed inches clear of Zeke's head.

Zeke's gun, echoing Clegg's pistol discharge, held in a rock-steady hand, punched a shell into Clegg's chest. He didn't fire a second load. Though Zeke knew he was no fast draw man he also knew that he was more accurate with a pistol or a long gun than most men. Clegg was still on his feet gazing in disbelief at the growing dark stain on his shirt. Then his look froze forever and Zeke watched him crumple at the knees and drop to the floor, his pistol rattling and sliding across the the boards, truly dead, with a great deal of satisfaction. He had sent a dyed-in-the-wool sinner, a man with murder in his black heart, to Hell and damnation where he belonged.

Stacey and Jed Logan, the only other Yankees in the gang, heard the two shots as they stepped on to the porch of the Long Branch. They exchanged, 'What the hell?' glances as they pushed their way through the swing doors just in time to see Clegg drop to the boards, and the man who had put him down standing on his own at the bar.

Logan cursed, and reached for his pistol. Stacey, with a whispered, 'Hold it!' put a restraining hand on Logan's arm. Logan shrugged it off and had half-drawn his gun when there came a shout from the bar owner of, 'The ruckus is over, boys, step up to the bar, drinks are on the house! Milligan, get that dead fella outa here!'

The saloon came alive again as men rushed to the bar for the offered drinks, some crowding round Zeke to congratulate him for his bold stand against the big gunman. A scowling-faced Logan thrust his gun back into its holster; he could no longer draw a bead on the man who had killed his blood cousin.

'I know Clegg was kin to you, Logan,' Stacey said, 'and you're naturally beholden to shoot the man who killed him. But not here, not in front of the sheriff. We'll bushwhack the sonuvabitch out on the street when he's on his own.' He had lost one man of his gang; he didn't want to lose another. He could maybe lose the whole gang if the 'breeds joined in the gun play. He looked across at them but he had been worrying for nothing. He could see no signs on their faces that they were about to yank out their guns and cut loose in what he reckoned they thought was gringo trouble.

'We've got a good thing goin' here for us, Logan,' Stacey continued. 'Don't ruin it for the rest of the boys by goin' off at half-cock. Start an unprovoked gunfight with a stranger and you'll be charged with murder, that's if you come out on top. The sonuvabitch who downed Pete must be good, m'be too good to meet face to face. Wait until he leaves the saloon and gun him down from some side alley where you'll have all the edge. Come on, let's join the boys at the table until it's time for you to go and settle the debt you owe Pete.' Personally Stacey didn't think that anyone owed Clegg any damn thing, the loud-mouthed bastard had got himself killed by calling out the wrong man.

'Yeah, I reckon you're right,' Logan said grudgingly. 'That fella's dead but he don't know it yet. Let's go and get our free drink.'

Sheriff Blakemore, who had kept himself low at the rear of the saloon out of harm's way of any stray Colt loads flying around when the two started shooting, assured Zeke that he had acted in self-defence, that the big, prodding bastard had drawn first, and for no reason at all.

'Finish your drink, son,' he said. 'And grab yourself a free one.' He grinned. 'You're the only fella in the place that deserves one. That was the slickest piece of gun-play I've seen in a long time.'

Zeke gave a weak grin. The reaction of the killing of his first man was giving him a sickly feeling in the pit of his stomach. Taking another pull at the whiskey would bring that sickness right into his mouth.

'I have to stay sober, Sheriff,' he replied. He nodded towards the 'breeds table. 'He was playing cards with that bunch; he could have been friendly enough with them for them to come after me. When things settle down here I'll sneak out by the back door and ride out of town, fast.'

One thing was for sure, a despondent Zeke thought, his grand plan of trailing the suspect raiders was no longer an option; they would be trailing him, and as slick with his gun as the sheriff thought he was, he couldn't take them all on and win through. He would have to ride back to the Paxton farm and tell Marshal Houseman that he had failed in his mission, though through no fault of his own. Zeke prayed that Bear Paw had better luck than he had had in picking up intelligence regarding the whereabouts of the raiders. He kept a wary-eyed gaze on the 'breeds, now, he noticed, joined by an anglo, ready, when he judged it right, to sneak out of the saloon. Choose the wrong time and he could find himself dead.

Bear Paw had left his horse tied up in a stand of timber and brush south of Bitter Water Springs to come into town on foot, acting the part of a drunken Indian, though he had his pistol stuffed down the top of his pants, the butt hidden by his fringed hide shirt.

He had picked up no solid information about the raiders from the Indian whose farm had just been attacked or from other farmers who had had their barns and homes burnt down by the night riders. He had been told that just before the raiding had started up a land agent, a white man, working out of Bitter Water Springs, had approached the raided farmers offering to buy their holdings at prices well below their true value.

Bear Paw didn't think that a land agent seeking to make easy money by buying cheap and selling dear was worth reporting back to Marshal Houseman. He felt it was beholden on him to ride on to Bitter Water Springs to see how Marshal Butler was faring, knowing the boy had made him a man again. Zeke hadn't the experience of handling hard men such as Marshal Houseman had and could easily land himself into a whole heap of trouble and would welcome help. Bear Paw smiled wryly – which wouldn't be much coming from a newly sobered up drunk.

Indian style he sneaked up to the livery barn and peered through the open doors. By the light of a lantern hanging from a post he saw Zeke's horse in one of the stalls which meant the boy was still in town seeking out information about the raiders. And the only place he could do any seeking was in the only saloon in town. Bear Paw smiled freely this time. Knowing Zeke's views on the evils of drinking, going into a saloon must be like taking a trip into his hell.

Logan had his free drink but didn't join Stacey as he made for the 'breed's table: he stayed at the bar. He had an itchy trigger finger, wanting to pull off a load at the son-of-a-bitch who had gunned down Clegg, whose reflection he could see in the bar mirror standing at the other end of the bar. And what riled him still further was that Clegg had been beaten to the draw by a moon-faced kid.

His watching paid off as he saw the kid cast a quick look towards Stacey's table before turning from the bar and making for the rear of the saloon. Logan gave a 'cat's-got-the-cream' gloating smile as he hurried across to the swing doors.

'Do you want help?' Stacey asked, as Logan came by his table.

'Nah,' replied Logan. 'The bastard's all mine!'

'When you down him, do it quietly, and well away from the saloon, *comprende*?' Stacey warned. 'They know that Clegg was sitting at this table and if their hero is found dead close by we'll have the law breathin' down our necks, trouble we don't want.' Trouble, he could have told Logan, Clegg's wild-ass action could have sicced on them.

Zeke didn't know he was heading into danger. He had reached the end of the alley running alongside the saloon with no sounds in the darkness behind him of any pursuing footsteps. He paused for a moment or two on the edge of Main Street to look along the porch of the saloon for any signs of the hard-faced 'breeds bursting out of the batwings. The three men who came staggering out, arms around each others' shoulders, singing their heads off, ranch-hands he thought, didn't pose a threat to him. He turned left and with some haste made for the livery barn.

Logan slipped from behind the three drunks and in several quick strides caught up with the man he would take great pleasure in killing.

Zeke gave a sharp gasp of pain as a knife point dug into his ribs and he heard a grating voice say, 'Just keep walkin', kid, or you'll get the rest of the blade pushed into you!'

Zeke stiffened up with alarm but kept on walking. It wasn't in his nature to curse himself for his foolishness in thinking that the man he had shot had no more companions than the four 'breeds and the American who had joined them. Instead, he did some rapid thinking of how he could get the better of the knife-wielding man without ending up dead in the process. An act he had to do on his own, unless he was blessed with a small miracle. Otherwise his first solo assignment as a US marshal would be his last.

Zeke saw the faint shape of a man coming along the boardwalk towards him, bobbing and swaying with every step he took. He felt another dig in his side with the knife and the warning of, 'Don't even think of it, kid,' from Logan. Logan gave out with a hoarse laugh. 'The sonuvabitch won't be able to help you, he's as drunk as a goddamned skunk.'

The drunk made his tanglefooted way past Zeke, his face covered by a drooping-brimmed hat, but Zeke clearly heard the soft chanting of a mournful Indian lament. He gave a slow relieved sigh, his unasked-for miracle was about to happen.

Logan had only time to growl, 'Outa the way, you drunken Injun!' when his head exploded in pain, then blackness overwhelmed him as he crashed down on to the boardwalk.

Zeke grabbed hold of Bear Paw's arm. 'He – he had a knife at my back, Mr Bear Paw. I was as good as dead if you hadn't showed up!' he gasped.

'How did you get—?'

'There's no time to tell you now, Beer Paw!' Zeke interrupted. 'That fella you laid out has a table full of hard-case friends back there in the saloon, all wanting to shed my blood. Let's get mounted up and ride out of town then I'll tell you the mess I've made of things here.'

When they were well clear of the town they eased back on their mounts and a now fully composed Zeke began to tell Bear Paw of the trouble that had flared up in the saloon, of his inner feeling that the four 'breeds and the American at the table might be the men they were searching for and how he was going to discover more about them by following them when they left the saloon so he could prove if his suspicions were right or wrong.

'Then for no reason at all the American picked a gunfight with me,' Zeke continued. Zeke's face steeled over. 'And I was forced to kill him, or he would have gunned me down! And that put an end to my trailing of the gang,' he added bitterly. 'I figured that once I left the saloon they would try and kill me for putting paid to their *compadre*, and I judged right. That fella you cold-cocked jumped me as soon as I came out into the alley.' He shot a quizzical glance at Bear Paw. 'What made you ride here, did you know I was in trouble?'

'Just by chance, Marshal,' replied Bear Paw. 'I picked up no information from the farmers I questioned for me to report back to Marshal Houseman, so I came to Bitter Water Springs just to see if you had better luck than me in your asking around. I caught sight of you with a man close behind on the boardwalk from across the street. By the store lights I could see by your look that you were not walking with him willingly. I ran back the way I had come, crossed over the street and acted the way I used to do.' Bear Paw grinned. 'Before you showed me the evil of my ways. It fooled that knife man long enough for me to give him one big headache when he comes to.'

Zeke got the chills again thinking of just how lucky he'd been. The miracle had been a big one. He muttered a belated 'thank you' prayer to the Almighty.

'We haven't much to report to Marshal Houseman,' Zeke said. 'And I've definitely overstayed my welcome here.'

'We did our best, Marshal,' Bear Paw replied. 'And it could have turned out a great deal worse.'

'I guess you're right,' Zeke said. 'M'be Marshal Houseman has had better luck than us. Let's find out!' He dug his heels into his horse's flanks.

By what Zeke had told him about the shoot-out in the saloon, Bear Paw thought, as he urged his own mount along, he was riding out with a full-blooded marshal – one Marshal Houseman should be proud to have as a partner.

ELEVEN

Marshal Houseman, squatting on the ridge above the Paxton farm, was doing his stint as a lookout. It was a spot well away from the good-living, God-fearing Paxton family's ears where he could do some serious cursing on himself for sending a young, newly sworn in marshal into a situation that had almost got him killed. His deputy and Bear Paw had ridden in half an hour ago, both of them telling him that their scouting expeditions hadn't come up with any firm leads on the raiders' whereabouts.

'I spotted a bunch of 'breeds and an American sitting at a table in the saloon,' Zeke had said. 'They had the hard-faced looks of owlhoots so I intended to track them when they left the saloon just to check them out.'

'I reckon the saloon must have been crowded with suspicious-looking characters, Deputy,' Houseman said. 'Cattle-lifters, bank-robbers and suchlike bad-asses, bein' that most of the good growin' land is owned by Injuns – no offence to you, Bear Paw – the white-eyes ain't got any other lawful trade to follow to

95

raise their wherewithal.' He looked back at Zeke. 'Did you manage to trail those 'breeds, Deputy?'

Zeke lowered his gaze. 'No, I didn't, Marshal. I was forced into a gunfight with the American who was with the 'breeds. Unfortunately I killed him.'

Houseman's eyes popped.

'The sheriff said it was in self-defence,' Zeke continued. 'So he's pressing no charge against me. But I thought it wise for me to get out of Bitter Water Springs as soon as I could before the 'breeds took it in their heads to avenge their *compadre's* death. I sneaked out of the back door of the saloon just as the American joined the 'breeds at their table. But another American I hadn't seen was waiting for me outside the saloon with a knife in his hand. I took him to be with the 'breeds and he was going to put paid to me. Then by some sort of a miracle Bear Paw showed up and cold-cocked him. Saving my life I reckon. Both of us agreed that I couldn't now operate in secrecy in Bitter Water Springs so we rode back here to see if you'd had better luck discovering who and where the raiders are holed up.'

Marshal Houseman's jaw dropped open. He was lost for words. His greenhorn deputy had shot down a border roughneck and escaped being knifed by a whisker, all told in a matter-of-fact voice as if the trouble he had come through was an everyday occurance. He was an unGodly-thinking man but someone, or something, had guided an ex-drunk heathen to Bitter Water Springs to save the kid's life. That would pass for a miracle in his book.

Finding his voice, he said, 'You did right to ride back

here, boys. Tanglin' with a bunch of *pistoleros* wasn't in your remit.' He grinned. 'And there's no need to look so down in the mouth. I ain't had any joy pickin' up the barn burners tracks and I've been out there searchin' for their sign almost every daylight hour. Now go and see to your horses then get freshened up. I'll ask Mrs Paxton to fix you up with some of her fine cooked vict-uals. And that means you as well, Bear Paw.' He grinned at Zeke. 'Sarah Jane will be mighty pleased to see you, Deputy. She'll make sure her ma feeds you well.'

Zeke lowered his head and gave out with a muttered, 'Ah heck, Marshal,' as he led his horse to the barn with the bow-shouldered, wide-footed stride of a ploughboy.

Houseman saw him in a different light. He knew the boy wasn't a trigger-happy hot head, seeking out trou-ble for a rep, yet it seemed when pushed into a corner he had acted with deadly efficiency. He was a natural born thief-taker; Judge Parker would be proud of him, as he was, but he'd be damned if he was going to tell the kid that.

Bear Paw grinned at Houseman. 'Marshal Butler isn't used to having a pretty young girl fussing over him.'

'Me neither,' Houseman grunted. 'Bein' one of Judge Parker's lawmen don't bring a heap of pleasure a fella's way. The boy wants to enjoy what joy he can grab hold of.' He hard-eyed Bear Paw. 'I could have been ridin' into that town to pick up his body. I owe you, Bear Paw, for savin' me that soulful trip.'

'There's no need to, Marshal,' Bear Paw said,

redman-faced. 'We deputies have to look out for each other.' Then he grinned as he grabbed hold of his horse's reins and followed Zeke to the stable.

Houseman shook his head. He couldn't have two finer men to ride the line with even if he had hand picked them.

As he walked across to the high ground he heard Bear Paw call over his shoulder that he had been told about a land agent from Bitter Water Springs who was offering to buy out the Indian farmers before they had been raided. It was news that aroused Houseman's interest enough to be chewed over while he was up on the ridge.

Cursing time was over, Houseman decided, decisions had to be made. His deputy, through no fault of his own, had failed to come up with a lead on Mr Stacey, the man who was hiring gunmen. Though now they had another possible lead to the raiders, a land agent. It was natural for a land agent to seek out land for sale, buying low and selling high was the way the mealy-mouthed swine did business. But a land agent who happened to call on farms that were later visited by the raiders set Houseman's lawman's highly tuned senses bristling. The raiders could be his method of persuading farmers to sell up. Hired gunmen cost money, more than a town land agent would have in the bank so the men footing the bill could be some Eastern big shots.

It would be worthwhile having a few words with this agent, Houseman thought, hard words, either to link him with the raiders or clear him. Then find Stacey and ask him the same questions. This raiding business had to be settled, pronto, no more pussyfooting around, concluded Houseman.

He hoped the Paxtons would see it his way and understood he was not running out on them, not when he had told Adam Paxton to expect another visit from the night riders. Houseman reckoned that the farmer would realize that he and his deputies couldn't stay here for any great length of time. Though understanding why wouldn't ease Paxton's worries about his family's well-being when the raiders came again. Houseman's lips hardened. He had made up his mind. The raiders had to be shot down a longways from the Paxton farm, then no one here would come to harm.

Houseman heard a slight rustling behind him and before he could twist round and see who had joined him on the ridge Bear Paw was standing over him.

'For a so-called civilized Injun, Mr Bear Paw,' Houseman growled good-naturedly, 'you sure move around as cat-footed as your wild brothers.'

A grinning Bear Paw sat down alongside him. 'If I hadn't been civilized, Marshal, you would have been minus what hair you've got left on your head.'

'I'm glad you're here,' Houseman said, then told Bear Paw of his intention to ride to Bitter Water Springs and bring things to a head. 'So your services as a temporary deputy ain't no longer needed,' he continued. 'Though if you hadn't been willin' to ride with me and the boy I wouldn't be sittin' here talkin' to you. You saved my skin once and my deputy's twice so I'll always be beholden to you, Bear Paw. Now you ride out to where you've decided to put down your roots.' He favoured Bear Paw with a stern-eyed fatherly look. 'Don't drift back to White Oaks and take up with your old habit again, *compadre*. Me and my deputy don't want to be passin' by that way again with the tumbleweed wagon to haul you outa town before that fella Madison plugs you.'

'As Deputy Butler would say, Marshal,' replied Bear Paw, 'I've seen the light.' Serious-voiced, he added, 'How will Mr Paxton take it when you tell him you're leaving, Marshal?'

'He'll not be overjoyed, that's for sure,' said an equally grave-voiced Houseman. 'Me neither, but me and the boy can't stay here waitin' for the raiders to show up just because of my gut feelings. I've got to move on. These raiders ain't the only bad-asses in the territory I've got to contend with.' Houseman gave a weary sigh. 'Judge Parker's laid a heavy load on my shoulders.' He heaved himself up on to his feet and gave Bear Paw a wry grin. 'I reckon it's time I told Mr Paxton the bad news.'

'I'll stay and take over the watch, Marshal,' Bear Paw said. Houseman's news that he and his deputy were riding on to Bitter Water Springs had suddenly presented him with some decisions he had to make. Decisions, drunk or sober, a puzzled Bear Paw thought he would never be called on to make. He hoped that a few other Cherokees would see the situation as he saw it or he would be up one damn muddy creek.

Houseman and Zeke were mounted up ready to ride out. Bear Paw, after handshakes and 'good lucks' from everyone, was already well along the trail. He'd left in a kicked-up, dust-raising gallop which made Houseman think that Bear Paw had had his fill of helping out white-eyed lawmen and was getting far away from them fast. Which disappointed him somewhat, being that he and the boy had built up a friendship with Beat Paw.

It wasn't the happiest of partings though Paxton knew that Marshal Houseman was making the right decision in going after the raiders. He couldn't expect them to stay at the farm indefinitely. It wasn't happy for Sarah Jane. On hearing, not from Zeke, that he'd killed a man in a gunfight then almost been knifed to death by another member of the gang, worried her sick. Even more so when Zeke told her that he and Marshal Houseman were leaving the farm to track down the raiders. She had never had such disturbing thoughts about a boy before. Could she have fallen in love with a ploughboy? Whatever it was, it gave her sufficient courage to reach up on her toes and kiss him full on the lips before he swung into his saddle.

'Don't fret about us, Marshal,' Adam Paxton said, with more conviction than he was feeling. He didn't want his family to know how low he was. 'We whupped them once, by thunder we'll do it again.'

Houseman didn't tell him that they had caught the raiders by surprise. The next time the sons-of-bitches rode in they'd come in Indian style, silently and fast, burn down the shack before the Paxtons knew they were under attack. Like Paxton he kept his bad feelings to himself.

'I reckon you can, Mr Paxton,' he said. 'But keep a sharp lookout at all times.' He gave the Paxtons a false confident grin. 'Between us we ought to put paid to those raiders in no time at all. And thanks for the fine chow you laid before me and my deputies.'

'You come by this way again once you've done what you came here to do, Marshal Houseman,' Mrs Paxton said. 'And me and Sarah Jane will cook something special for you.'

Final 'So longs' were said and Houseman and Zeke dug their heels into their mounts' ribs, setting them on the trail to Bitter Water Springs. And Sarah Jane ran inside the shack, sobbing.

Houseman looked across at the glum-faced Zeke. As well as having religion it seemed that his deputy was suffering from a hefty dose of love sickness – a state of mind he didn't want his back-up gun to be cursed with; it could get them both killed. Houseman directed a few more silent curses Judge Parker's way.

It had been thirty-six hours since Houseman and Zeke had left the Paxtons to fend on their own. Thirty-six hours of nail-biting anxiety for all of the Paxtons. Adam and Sarah Jane were feeding the stock, Mrs Paxton was busy in the shack preparing an evening meal, Dave doing duty as the lookout. Every now and again a nerve-taut Paxton looked up at the ridge dreading Dave's warning cry of, 'Riders coming in!' He hoped the boy hadn't fallen asleep; both of them had been on watch most of the night. Ma and Sarah Jane spelling them for an hour or so while they drank cups of strong black coffee or snatched a few minutes' of eyeball-easing sleep.

The lookout post on the high ground hadn't been manned during the night. Paxton dared not risk having David being cut off from the house if the raiders came in after dark. Following the basic rules of warfare, bloodily learned during the Civil War, Paxton wanted to concentrate his fire power in face of the enemy. Fire power! He gave a derisive snort. Some power – two Winchesters, a pistol and a single-barrelled shotgun. His position if the worst came to the worst was in the loft of the big barn where from the hoist opening he had a clear view of the front of the house – the killing ground. The crossfire would cover the house, from David with the other rifle, Ma with his old army Dragoon pistol and Sarah Jane armed with the shotgun, gainst his strong wishes that she should seek shelter in the root cellar if the raiders came. Her bold statement of, 'I'm part of this family as well, Pa!' brought tears of pride to his eyes. Pride, Paxton thought bitterly, that may well get them all killed. Cold logic told him that they hadn't a cat in hell's chance of beating off eight or ten well-armed men determined to burn them out; they could only make them pay dearly with their own dirty blood.

David's cry of, 'Riders comin' in!' increased the despondent thoughts in his mind, the killing time had arrived. But he had to show strength of purpose in front of his family. He grabbed hold of his rifle and dashed out of the barn.

'Into the house, Sarah Jane!' he yelled. 'And you and your ma keep your heads down! David will join you in a minute!'

Then he heard David's call of, 'It's OK, Pa, It's Bear Paw leadin' them!' had Paxton casting his daughter a puzzled but highly relieved look.

Bear Paw and four riders swept round the southern edge of the high ground just as David came scrambling down from the ridge to join him. Only Bear Paw came right up to them, the other riders drew up their mounts in a loose half-circle thirty feet or so from the house.

'My uncle and two of his sons have come with me, Mr Paxton,' Bear Paw said. 'We will stand guard on your land until Marshal Houseman and Deputy Butler return from Bitter Water Springs. That's if you are willing to accept our help.'

Paxton took a long look at Bear Paw's uncle and his cousins. Though, unlike Bear Paw, they wore sober-coloured store suits, his uncle even sporting a hard hat, they had the stone-faced looks of uncivilized hair-lifting broncos.

'Their farm was raided two nights ago,' Bear Paw continued. 'They know that you are the only farmer who has beat off the raiders and killed many of them. When I told my uncle that you could be raided again he thought that it was only right he should come here with his sons to get the chance of regaining his lost pride at allowing some white-eyed bandits to destroy his home by shooting down some of the raiders.

'I'm mighty pleased to accept your uncle and his boys help,' Paxton replied. 'Mighty pleased.' If he had been a crying man Paxton would have burst into tears of joy. 'You and your kin can step down, Bear Paw. See that their horses are watered, David!' Turning to face his wife and daughter standing on the porch he said, 'Get some coffee goin' for our neighbours, Ma.'

TWELVE

Marshal Houseman caught sight of the straggling line of shacks on the outskirts of Bitter Water Springs and drew up his mount; Zeke did likewise.

'This is the closest I dare risk gettin' to Bitter Water Springs along an open trail in daylight, Deputy,' he said. 'Any moment some fella ridin' into or outa town could come along. A fella who knows me, friendly or otherwise, and in no time at all, believe me, it will be big news that two of Judge Parker's manhunters are roamin' about the territory and the men we're seekin' will go to ground. You'll have to ride in on your own to find out where that land agent works from.'

He grinned. 'You'll be well known as a fast gun *hombre*, not as a marshal.' Houseman's face grimmed over. 'But that don't mean you can swagger along Main Street like some bold *pistolero*. You could meet up with that knifeman again, bring a whole heap of grief on your head. Make enquiries about the land agent at the livery barn; it's at this end of the town, OK? I'll keep low in that dry wash across the trail there till you show up.'

'OK, Marshal,' replied Zeke. He didn't need Marshal Houseman warning him to watch out for trouble in Bitter Water Springs. He had been lucky in his gunfight with the big man in the saloon and he firmly believed that a miracle, worked through Bear Paw, had saved him from being knifed to death. He couldn't pray and expect another miracle would come his way if he faced bad trouble again.

Well within the hour Zeke was on his way back from his mission and after making sure that the way ahead, and behind him, was deserted he cut across the trail to meet up with Houseman waiting in the wash.

'The land agent, Mr Frazer,' Zeke began, 'has an office at the far end of Main Street, a building set back on its own. Though he won't be open for business until he comes back in from his regular morning ride.'

Houseman gave a satisfied grunt. 'Good work, Deputy. We'll circle the town and come on his place by the back door.' Houseman's grin was a cold all-toothed grimace. 'And ask him some pointed questions about his land purchasin' deals. We'll—'

'Rider coming along the trail, Marshal,' interrupted Zeke and led his horse deeper into the wash.

The rider, coming from the town, looking straight ahead, passed them at a steady trot.

'Well I'll be durned!' Zeke gasped. 'That fella joined the 'breeds in the saloon just after the gunfight.'

'Did he now?' replied Houseman thoughtfully. 'It will be worth our while to trail that fella, see where he leads us to. If he meets up with the 'breeds then we can take it that the sonsuvbitches are a gang. What mischief they're gangin' up to do might not be so easy to discover. I know we're grabbin' at straws to find out where the raiders hole-up, Deputy, but there ain't no other way for us to try.'

Stacey had no idea he was being tailed. He was trying to think of the reason why Frazer wanted to see him. The raiding was still going smoothly, none of his boys had even suffered so much as a scratch.

He had been on his way to the eating-house to have his breakfast when Frazer, starting his morning ride, slow walked his horse past him and gave him a mean-ingful glance before heeling his horse into a liver-shak-ing trot. Whatever reason Frazer wanted him for it would wait until he had eaten. Rolling about in bed most of the night with the young blonde gave a man an appetite.

Frazer had dismounted and was pacing up and down the front of the broken-down building, his temper well over the boiling point at Stacey's late arrival. He was mad angry enough that once Striker gave the order to cease the raiding he would take the pistol he had in the top drawer of his desk and blow Stacey's head off so the son-of-a-bitch wouldn't be able to enjoy spending the good money he had been paying him.

Some of his rage he vented on Striker. The wire he had received from him had simply stated: URGENT. SPEED UP THE PROCESS. CASH TO COVER ADDITIONAL EXPENSES FOLLOWING. STRIKER. Frazer could understand the reason for the wire, the date for the opening of the Strip to thousands of land-seeking Easterners wasn't far away and the Indian Land Development Company wanted to own as much land as it could. But did the fat, well-fed bastard want a whole army of raiders driving out every goddamned Indian farmer, Frazer thought? His earlier fears returned. It only needed one of Stacey's cut-throats to be captured while raiding a farm and finger Stacey as the gang leader and Stacey, with a handful of dead or alive warrants posted on him, would name him as the man who had paid for the raids to save his dirty neck from being stretched by the hanging rope.

When at last Stacey pulled up at the broken-down shack and dismounted, Frazer kept his black thoughts to himself. The shut-faced Western breed of men frightened him. At the slighest slur against their misguided sense of pride they would pull out their long-barrelled pistols and proceed to shoot lumps out of each other, even men they classed as their partners, so instead he told Stacey about the urgent need to step up the raiding. Anticipating Stacey's first question he added, 'I ought to have the extra cash you'll need to hire more men in a day or two.'

Houseman and Zeke, lying low behind a fold in the ground, watched the two talking.

'That dude must be the land agent we've come here to have a word with, Deputy,' Houseman said. 'And there he is, chattin' away with a man who is pals with a bunch of mixed-blood *pistoleros* and a coupla gringos, men who tried to kill you. I'd bet my last dollar that he's Mr Stacey, the fella Belle Starr told us about, him who's hirin' hard men.' Houseman thought for a few minutes before speaking again. 'If we can Injun up on them close enough to hear what they're yappin' about we could find out for sure if they're involved in the farm-burnin' business. Though as you know, Judge Parker's law don't hold sway this side of the line, that don't stop me as a concerned citizen calling them out and accusing them of law-breakin' and shootin' them down where they stand if they want to take the hard way out.'

Shoot them down in cold blood? A shocked Zeke eyeballed Houseman. Was the old marshal ribbing him? He saw no sigh of humour in the blood-darkened, flint-eyed gaze. He swallowed hard. He had just learned something else serving as a peace officer in Indian Territory. Sometimes he would have to act as judge, jury and executioner. In this wild land he would be tracking down men, life-long sinners who could never be granted the Christian charity of being given the benefit of the doubt.

He heard Houseman growl, 'Damn, there's a bunch of riders comin' along the trail causin' those two sonsuvbitches to cut short their meetin'. Look, they're mountin' up and ridin' back to town! It's back to our original plan, Deputy, of payin' a call on that shyster. We've got something on him now. I'll squeeze him till he tells us why he's consortin' with a man who keeps bad company. OK, let's make that call.'

They both got to their feet and made for their horses.

Frazer had cut away from the main trail, not wanting to be seen within rifle range of Stacey this close to town, which gave Stacey time to think of where he could raise up a bigger gang, quickly. He would find the men for sure, the cash was there for the taking. In all his bank and stage-heisting days he had never raked in so much of the wherewithal. It was like money from home.

THIRTEEN

Zeke heard another, 'Goddamn and blast!' from Marshal Houseman. Blasphemy and strong oaths were a burden he had to get used to being a US marshal. Houseman wanted to come out with real mule-skinner cursing words but didn't want his Christian-minded deputy to have a low opinion of him by thinking that he was partnered with a foul-mouthed character. If the kid caught him sneaking a pull at the whiskey bottle, or enjoying the pleasures of a woman outside of Holy wedlock why he'd probably quit the marshalling business and haul himself back to his pa's farm. Which, Houseman thought, wouldn't be a bad idea, the boy would live to an old age and be able to sit on his front stoop watching his grandchildren at play.

They had ridden well clear of Bitter Water Springs to come on the town from the west trail, the quieter end of the town and where Zeke had been told the land agent had his place of business. What had caused Houseman's outburst was seeing the agent ushering an elderly man and woman into his office. Which meant that they had to stay in town longer than he had wanted, risking being spotted as lawmen, then bang would go the far reaching possibility of sneaking up on the night raiders. Houseman's 'damns and blasts' were muttered under his breath this time. Aloud he said, 'We'll just have to hangfire our chat with that shyster a spell, Deputy. Until it's OK for us to walk in and consult with him.' He fierce-grinned Zeke. 'For free!'

'That will give me time to go along to the livery barn and have the smith fix my horse's loose shoe,' Zeke said.

'OK, Deputy, you do that,' Houseman replied. 'But there's a few more citizens on the street along that end of the town so keep your wits about you. Remember we ain't supposed to be here.'

'Your horse needs a new shoe, boy,' Jeb Grant, the smithy said. 'I could nail the old one back on but after a coupla hours or so of hard ridin' the horse would throw it and you could have a lame animal on your hands.'

'I guess it will have to be done then,' Zeke said. 'Will it take long? I'm in a kinda hurry.' Though he was thinking that as the smithy hadn't recognized him as the winner in the saloon shoot-out here in the livery barn would be a good place to lie low in until his horse had been seen to.

'Not long at all,' Grant said. 'As soon as I put a few rivets in this saddle strap I'll get on to re-shoeing your horse.'

Zeke waited until the smithy began working on his horse then he walked to the door to keep a watchful eye on the comings and goings on Main Street and walked straight into big trouble, in the shape of one of the 'breeds whom he thought could be members of the gang doing the raiding.

Urbino, who had come to the barn to see if his saddle had been repaired, got over his surprise meeting first. Cursing, he snatched out his gun and triggered off two loads as wildly as he had drawn his pistol. The shells whizzed harmlessly over Zeke's right shoulder and winged their way into the barn. The smithy flung himself face down on to a heap of raked-up straw and horse droppings as the shells kicked splinters off a wooden post close by his head. Zeke, strangely feeling no fear or panic, brought his gun into play and his single head shot killed the 'breed before he could thumb back the hammer of his pistol for a third shot. As the 'breed collapsed to the ground there came a crack of another pistol and Zeke gasped with pain as a shell sliced through the thick flesh of his upper arm with the burning sharpness of a fire-heated blade. He swung round to face his new danger, another of the 'breeds, at the corner of a building way up the alley from the barn, taking aim at him again.

Zeke's pain-blurred vision prevented him from making his second kill but his fusillade of shots forced the 'breed to draw back behind the building, out of sight, giving him time to make his next move. He had used up all his pistol loads and if he slipped back into the barn to reload, the 'breed would close in on him and pick him off as he showed himself once more. It was time, Zeke thought grimly, to cut and run for it, on foot. He couldn't move fast up on a horse wearing only three shoes. He smiled. Marshal Houseman would call it 'getting the hell out of it'.

Low-backed, Zeke sped along the alley and darted into the first of the empty back lots running the length of the rear of Main Street just as he heard the whanging sound of a shell striking a metal structure and its blood-chilling ricocheting above his head.

The empty lots were a tangled wildness of thick patches of brush and tall thickets, though with a track of sorts snaking round the undergrowth. To use the way he had ridden along to get to the livery barn now would be presenting himself as a clear target to his attacker. Cover not speed would keep him alive.

The brush tore at his clothes, impeding his flight, and causing extra pain to his wounded arm. He guessed by the swaying of the brush and thickets as he ploughed through them the 'breed would be able to follow his trail though not clear enough to take a direct shot at him. Two shots which came nowhere near him proved his guess a fact.

The brush patch began to thin out and Zeke caught sight of an opening between two buildings twenty or so yards ahead of him; a way to make it to Main Street. Too open, maybe, Zeke thought, for his pursuer to continue shooting at him. Also it was where Marshal Houseman was waiting for him. Then, by heck, he told himself, if the 'breed wanted a gunfight he would get one.

Zeke cleared the stretch of open ground to the mouth of the alley in a series of high stepping jumps, shells punching holes in a timber post of the building he was cornering, giving him that extra burst of life-saving speed.

Part way down the alley, a door swung open in a building to his left and a girl stepped out and grabbed hold of his arm.

'In here, ploughboy,' she said. 'You're about to run into most of the Stacey gang, friends of the sonuvabitch who's shootin' at you!'

Before Zeke could say otherwise he was bundled inside the building. Though he wasn't that taken aback not to notice that the girl was barefooted and dressed only in a loose-fitting shift that barely reached her knees; and he had never heard a female call a man a sonuvabitch before.

The dimly lit passage way was narrow forcing Zeke to stand close to the girl, near enough to feel the heat from her body and the throat-catching smell of her perfume. Then the realization of his strange situation became clear. He was in the house of ill-repute and his would-be rescuer, a fallen dove. Or, as his pa would say, a scarlet woman, a whore. A sinner who would only get redemption on Judgement Day. Yet a sinner, Bear Paw, a former drunkard and not even a Christian, had saved his life. Now it looked like a girl who sold her body for money had done the same. Maybe, he thought, he shouldn't be so unbending in his attitude towards sinners as his pa had taught him to be.

He started to ask the girl about the gang leader, Stacey, she had mentioned, when she put a finger on his lips to silence him. Zeke heard the sound of footsteps in the alley then the rattling of the door handle. He silently thanked the girl for using her wits by bolting it. Quickly, he thumbed reloads into his pistol and with it held at full-cock he aimed it at the door in case it was kicked open. Face grim set he was prepared to make his stand here; he had finished running.

The girl in her fear pressed closer to Zeke, the warm softness of her unfettered breasts brushing against him. Zeke flinched visibly and felt a tightness at his throat and a vein pounded in his temple. Yet it wasn't an unpleasant feeling and for a brief spell of time he forgot the deadly threat beyond the door.

'Er, you'd better go upstairs, miss,' he croaked hoarsely. 'There's no need for that gunman out there to know that you've helped me.'

'Why, you're wounded, mister!' the girl said ignoring his plea.

'Not mister, miss, Marshal, Marshal Butler,' Zeke replied proudly. 'And it's only a flesh wound. Now go. I'll—'

'He's goin' away, Marshal!' the girl said, taking no notice of his order to go to her room.

Zeke's nerves began to unwind a little when he heard no sound of movement in the alley. Slowly he eased forward the hammer of the Colt and held it down by his side. He turned and glanced at the girl, then quickly averted his gaze at seeing so much naked female flesh.

'Now tell me about Stacey and the men who ride with him,' he said. He looked about him. 'Can we go someplace else to do the talking?' This close to the girl was unsettling him, preventing him from thinking clearly.

'No, we're safer here, ploughboy Marshal,' the girl replied mockingly. 'Blondie, one of the girls upstairs, is Stacey's favourite. The less she sees the less she can blab about to Stacey. By the way my name is Julie, that's if you're interested.' She grinned up at Zeke. 'If you come into the cat house by the front door next time, Marshal, I'll make you forget your troubles for a coupla hours or so.'

Zeke more than flinched. This time he stepped a full yard back from the girl. Was she deliberately trying to embarrass him? He remembered a girl shouting, 'countryboy' at him from the cat house as he came into town. Had it been the girl who was offering her body to him? Zeke began to panic, the sooner he got the information he sought the sooner he would meet up with Marshal Houseman, and the sooner his blood would cool down.

He thought of the sweet smiling Sarah Jane and mumbled something about being that he was kind of courting a farm girl he couldn't see himself paying a visit to the cat house. Then in a voice more resolute he said, 'Now about this fella Stacey?' and curious to why she had come to his aid he added, 'Why did you come out into the alley and help me, Julie?'

'Clegg, the man you shot in the saloon, Marshal,' Julie began, 'Was, if you don't already know, a member of Stacey's gang, like the 'breed who is tryin' to gun you down. That sonuvabitch Clegg beat me up the last time he paid a visit here. Said I didn't perform good enough for the cash he paid.' Zeke thought that he definitely hadn't to judge sinners too harshly. Even sinners, by what the girl had told him, were sinned against. 'So when I saw you from my window in my room at the back of the house I felt that, bein' you were headin' this way, it was beholden of me to help you out. I came out into the alley to see if the coast was clear just in time to see Stacey and Logan, one of his sidekicks, the fella who got himself cold-cocked, crossin' the top of the alley.' Julia gave Zeke a questioning look. 'Was it one of your buddies who bounced his pistol off Logan's thick skull? The whole bunch of them are no-good back-shooters. Anyway I knew that you would be runnin' into trouble if you made it to Main Street. Two guns in front of you, and one closin' in on you at the rear.' Julie grinned. 'So I dragged you in here.'

And God bless you for that charitable action, Zeke thought, with much fervour.

'This Stacey, is he boss over a real gang,' he asked, 'or are they all just drinking and card playing friends?'

Julie gave a snorting laugh. 'They all have money to toss around on gamblin', drinkin' and in here, and they sure haven't earned it nursin' cows on some ranch or ploughin' fields.'

Zeke studied Julie for a while before he spoke again. The girl had risked harm on his behalf, it was only right that she knew the reason why he was in Bitter Water Springs. Especially when she had already, unintentionally, got involved in his and Marshal Houseman's mission.

'What I'm about to tell you, Julie,' he said sober-voiced, 'is strictly between you and me, or you could be coming to my aid again, or seeing me buried.'

'I'm listenin', Marshal,' Julie replied, face as solemn-looking as Zeke's.

'I'm riding with Marshal Houseman,' Zeke said. 'We are two of Judge Parker's marshals sent here by the judge to put paid to the gang who's raiding the Indian farmers hereabouts. I've more than a strong feeling that Stacey and his gang are the raiders and by what you've just told me my guess was right. But me and Marshal Houseman have to be able to prove it in a court of law. Or shoot them down if they want to make a fight of it. If they get wind we're on their trail me and Marshal Houseman will have lost our only edge, surprise.'

Julie wanted to laugh outright. Two lawmen, one an open-faced farmboy, scared of partly clothed females, dressed up like some hillbilly, taking on Stacey and his mean-eyed 'breeds? The boy must have caught Clegg off-guard that night in the saloon. She had saved his life for a few more days that's all, Julie thought.

Then she heard the young marshal say, 'We've made a good start, as well as sending Clegg to Hell, where he was destined, I made one of the 'breeds pay the full price for his sinful ways.'

A slack jawed Julie gazed up at Zeke as though seeing him for the first time, which, when she thought about it, she really was. 'Sent to Hell where he belonged' and 'paying for his sinful ways', were sayings she remembered hearing as a child at church meeting days spoken by a hell and damnation circuit preacher. Noticing Zeke's wild-eyed look, she reckoned she was seeing a younger version of that preacher man. The kid had got religion bad. Stacey and his wild bunch had felt the wrath of God and were about to get another dose of it and she almost felt sorry for them. His scary look put her off from ribbing him any more.

'I'll go now, Miss Julie,' Zeke said. 'What with all the shooting going on Marshal Houseman will be worrying

119

about me. God bless you for coming to my aid.' He touched his hat in a farewell gesture.

Before he turned away, Julie said, 'I'd better take a look in the alley first, Marshal, just in case those sonsuv—, beggin' your pardon, Marshal.' Being blessed, even by a ploughboy, had Julie remembering that it was unladylike to use such coarse language. 'Er, just in case that 'breed hasn't quit huntin' you down,' she said instead.

'You've already paid the debt you said you reckon you owe me, miss,' Zeke said firmly. 'I don't want to put you into any further danger. It's mine and Marshal Houseman's business and that's the way I want Stacey to see it. He hasn't to know that we've had your help, OK?'

It had been a long, long time since a man had considered her anything more than a two-dollar hump, Julie thought; now here was a stranger, a mere wet-behind-the-ears kid, genuinely worried about her well-being, worried that she may come to harm. On a sudden, moist-eyed impulse she reached up on her toes and kissed Zeke full on the lips. The first real kiss for free she had given since becoming a short-time girl. And the second Zeke had been given from a female other than his mother.

Zeke was still savouring the unexpected experience as after a quick look up and down the alley he stepped outside. He heard a soft-voiced, 'Good luck, plough-boy,' behind him then the door being shut. He raised his pistol and became a lawman once more, prepared to gun down any sinner who dared to prevent him from upholding the law.

*

Houseman had tied up his horse at the rear of the agent's office and, taking out his rifle, had walked a short way along the street and sat down in the deep shadows of a boarded-up store's porch from where, without being observed himself, he could see the office for when it would be time to to make his call on him, and the comings and goings further along the street. If they had figured right that Stacey was the boss of the raiders then it meant that his gang were here in Bitter Water Springs, drinking in the saloon he hoped, until his deputy came back from the livery barn.

Then Houseman told himself he was acting like a fussy old maid worrying about his young deputy. He had told the boy to look out for himself and he had to trust him to do that. He had to allow him to make decisions on his own or he would never make a lawman. And up till now Deputy Butler had shown all the quick thinking and deadly action of a seasoned marshal. Though that assessment of his partner didn't stop Houseman wishing that the boy would soon show up.

'I've got another four men lined up, Logan,' Stacey said. The pair were bellied up to the saloon bar, the 'breeds sitting at their usual table playing poker. 'They're camped outside of town near Bull Run crossing,' he continued. He grinned. 'They're kinda unwelcome in town being that the sheriff here holds several warrants on them for various law-breakin' activities. You ride with them, Logan. I told them that they had to be ready to move out in a coupla hours' time.'

Stacey's face hardened. 'Me and the 'breeds' are goin' to even up the score with that sodbuster for killin' the boys. I know you'd like to be at the party, Logan, but someone has to boss over the new men, make sure they're worth their pay. We'll make certain that that sodbuster and his kin don't plant another corn seed or milk a cow ever again.'

Stacey saw Urbino and Orozco get up from the table and walk out of the saloon.

'Where the hell are those two going?' he growled at Logan. 'If they're payin' a call at the cat house and get themselves liquored before havin' a session with the girls we'll have to hog tie them to get them out.'

Logan grinned. 'Don't worry, they ain't got enough spendin' money left for them to pay a visit next door. Urbino, I reckon, is on his way to the livery barn. He's havin' some repairs done to his saddle gear. Orozco was tellin' me early on that he was runnin' short of Winchester shells so he could be goin' across the street to the store. They'll be ready to ride out when the time comes, Stacey; as I said they're runnin' short of cash.'

Stacey grunted. He hoped Logan had told him right. He had held all the different kinds of hell he was going to sic on the sodbuster and his family churning up inside him for far too long. He took another pull at his beer.

Houseman saw two men step out of the saloon. Men wearing high-steepled plains hats and wide bottomed pants. Sunlight winked off the shells in a belt that one of them had slung over his right shoulder. Though he couldn't make out their features he had a feeling in his gut that they were two of the 'breeds his deputy mentioned being part of Stacey's gang. The pair turned and walked away from him, in the general direction of the livery barn.

He stood up, cursing. His fears that his deputy could be running into trouble came flooding back. He didn't give a damn now about Judge Parker's suggestion that he should 'sneak' into Bitter Water Springs, not when his greenhorn deputy's life could be in danger. The whole goddamned town could see him.

Yet, Houseman thought, he could be having another attack of old maid's nerves. At this very moment his deputy could be riding across the back lots to meet up with him. But by his long experience as a lawman, and still above ground, Houseman knew that it didn't do any harm to think gloomy thoughts and prepare for the worst. He got to his feet and levered a shell into the chamber of his rifle and as casually as his screwed-up nerves allowed him he trailed the 'breeds. He hung back for several seconds when one of the gunmen crossed over to his side of the street and walked into the general store, the bandoleer-wearing 'breed kept on heading towards the livery barn.

The 'breed had hardly turned into the alley and out of his sight when Houseman heard gunfire. He cursed, his worst fears had been realized: his deputy had met up with trouble. He was just about to break into a run to back up the boy when the 'breed's partner rushed out of the store and hared across to the alley. Houseman paused to do some fast thinking, and some sure-fire cursing, on how he was going to help out his partner without charging bull-like against two professional guns and getting himself killed.

The 'breed who had been in the store was firing his pistol into the alley from the corner of a building fronting the street, which meant to a straw-clutching Houseman that his deputy was still alive. He brought his rifle up to his shoulder to back shoot the 'breed, an action that didn't upset Houseman's code of honour any. Men who robbed and killed innocent folk had to be dispatched to Boot Hill in the way the game played out, face to face, from ambushcade or whatever. Then he hesitated for a moment to take the shot.

He noticed that the shooting had brought men out on to the street. He didn't see the sheriff among them, but one of them could be his deputy. The lawman seeing a man aiming a rifle while a gunfight was taking place would throw down on him. Then it was too late for him to fire, his target had gone into the alley. The next shots Houseman heard sounded from the back lots. His deputy was still up and moving, and he had to get across there to keep him that way.

The four men who came out of the saloon and hurrying along the boardwalk put an abrupt end to going to his deputy's aid. Two of the men were 'breeds, the Yankees were Stacey and a beer-bellied hardcase. Houseman glimpsed the whiteness of a bandage showing beneath the fat man's hat. He cold grinned: Bear Paw's doing, he opined.

He lowered his rifle and stood well back in the shadows of the porch roof as they passed him and turned into the alley. Houseman wasn't a praying man but he mumbled a few words of a prayer of sorts for the safety of his Christian-minded deputy. He had failed his partner, he thought bitterly, only God could help him out now, if he took note of an old sinner's plea.

Stacey, as he hurried along, was in one hell of a temper. Standing with Logan at the bar and pleased with the quickness he had raised up a bunch of willing fire-raisers, he had heard the firing and didn't need a map to show him where it was taking place, and whose guns were doing some of the shooting, the trigger-happy Urbino and Orozco. Just when they were about to ride out and do what they had been paid good money to do, the crazy sons-of-bitches had got themselves into a gunfight. The four 'breeds had been a handful to control when they were not earning their due, downing rotgut whiskey tended to bring out their Apache fathers' wild blood. He looked behind him and saw that Silvero and Castro were already on their feet and making for the door.

'Let's go, Logan,' he grated. 'And try and keep them outa that trouble their pards seem to have stirred up at the far end of town or we'll be back to one gang again.'

Several worrying minutes later, Houseman saw the four of them coming back on to the street again, the two 'breeds part-carrying, part-dragging, a dirt-scuffing-heels body between them. Houseman gasped as though he had been dealt a blow with a fist. Then his eyes narrowed into red-streaked pinpoints of rage at the sons-of-bitches who had gunned down his deputy, the boy he was supposed to look out for. He brought his rifle waist high, reckoning that with the suddennness of his attack, he ought to put three of them down forever before he paid the price of his wild action.

Houseman suddenly stepped back from the edge of

the porch as he got a closer look at the body, and the belt of reloads draped across its chest. He grinned widely, his killing lust cooling down somewhat. His 'glory boy' charge wasn't needed. Deputy Marshal Butler was still alive and had proved his deadly skill with a gun again. His grin slipped slightly when he realized that there were four 'breeds in Stacey's gang, one was still out there, though he had heard no more shooting so he guessed that the kid had given him the slip.

Houseman had his reasoning proved right when the missing 'breed, the man who had been in the store, came out of the alley between the saloon and the cat house. A scowling-faced, disappointed-looking 'breed. Stacey and the fat Yankee stopped to have words with him as the other two men continued to haul their dead *compadre* along to the morticians. He couldn't hear what the 'breed was telling Stacey but opined that he was telling him who it was who had shot down the bandoleer man, and that he had cut and run for it.

Stacey, trying hard not to rile Orozco any more than he was right now after seeing his cousin shot down and his killer running free, was telling him that he would be wasting his time trying to hunt down the gringo kid.

'He'll be long gone by now, *amigo*,' he said. 'But that don't mean we ain't goin' to seek him out. I want the sonuvabitch to pay for shootin' down Clegg. Once we've done the coupla chores we've been paid to do I'll have the four new boys to give us a hand in tracking down the kid.' Stacey wondered briefly who the kid was. The territory was swarming with ragged-assed kids aiming to be fearsome *pistoleros*. This kid had already made the grade as a genuine gunman. If he hadn't shot Logan and Urbino he would have welcomed him into the gang.

He spoke again to Orozco, in mealy-mouthed sympathy. 'Though it's up to you and your *compadres* to do what you feel you oughta do, like kinda wantin' blood for blood. If you decide to go after the kid it'll upset the man who's hirin' us and our easy money days will be over.'

Stacey saw the madness begin to fade out of Orozco's eyes and breathed a silent sigh of relief. As he had banked on, the greed of easy-come-by money made the 'breed think of his real priorities. Avenging the killing of a distant relative came well down his list.

'Me and my *compadres* will ride with you, Stacey,' Orozco said. Then his black button eyes hardened again. 'But afterwards it will be our knives or bullets that kill the gringo *chico*.'

Stacey smiled. 'That's OK by me, *amigo*. When we rope him in you and your boys can work on him, Injun fashion.' He had told Orozco that he wanted the kid dead for his killing of Clegg but that didn't mean that he was going to rush into a face-to-face gunfight with a fast-draw shootist. His friendship with Clegg didn't go deep enough for suchlike mad-ass action. Unless he had all the edge he would gladly stand aside and let any of the 'breeds do the shooting.

As he watched Orozco walk along the street to the undertakers he thought that some good had come his way from the killing of Urbino. True he was now one man short but the shooting of one of their own blood had stirred up the 'breeds killing lust. He needed them in that blood-letting mood when he raided the sodbuster who had almost wiped out his first gang again.

'You get saddled up,' he told Logan. 'And go and meet up with your boys. Make sure they know what's expected of them.' He gave a mirthless all-toothed grin. 'I'll go back into the saloon and wait till the 'breeds have paid their last respects to Urbino then we'll hit the trail.'

The shooting had woken up Sheriff Blakemore, having his daily boots off *siesta* in one of the cells in his jailhouse. By the time, still half asleep, he had rolled off the cot and pulled on his boots and got out on to his stoop the shooting had ceased. He became fully awake when he saw two of Stacey's 'breeds hefting one of their own between them into Ben Douglas's funeral parlour.

He couldn't hear any more firing and as far as he could see there were no bodies lying in the street. Shooting scrapes were a common occurence in Bitter Water Springs and as long as the trigger-happy shootists didn't harm any innocent bystander or shoot up any property, and didn't last too long, he tended to let things run their course. Or he'd have to ask the mayor to build him a bigger jailhouse.

He held no warrants on Stacey or the men he bossed over, but he had more than just a feeling that they were the men behind the burning-out raids in the territory so he reckoned that whoever had shot down the 'breed had struck a blow for law and order in his bailiwick. Like that young kid had done by out-gunning Clegg in the saloon the other day. He took another look along the street, the few gawpers were heading back into their stores or the saloon. Satisfied that no more trouble was about to break out he stepped back into his office. He sat down on the bunk and eased off his boots again and was soon stretched out to drop off to sleep with the comforting thought that two less thieving sons-of-bitches were drinking in the saloon.

By this time Houseman was making his way back along the street to the land agent's office where he believed his deputy would be waiting for him, having successfully escaped being shot by the 'breeds. He suddenly stopped dead in his tracks when he spotted his deputy poke his head cautiously round the corner of the alley between the saloon and the cat house.

He waved his hand frantically to catch the attention of Zeke, too worried about how things could turn nasty to come out with his usual string of oaths when he was being pushed into a corner. If the kid slipped into the street the same time as the three 'breeds came out of the undertakers, or Stacey showed up on the saloon porch, then one hell of a gunfight would start up in Bitter Water Springs. He and his young deputy taking on several men. And that, he thought, with some dry humour, would have Sheriff Blakemore fire-balling out of his office with his suspenders dangling below his knees.

Zeke saw Marshal Houseman's warning signals and ducked back into the alley to continue his way to rendezvous with him at the office under the cover of the back lots. As he forced his way through the thick growing undergrowth, and between times of casting apprehensive glances behind him, Zeke reflected that in his short spell of being a state marshal he had wounded one man, seen two killed by Bear Paw and ended the lives of two men himself. He managed a weak grin. And had his life saved by a lady of ill repute.

FOURTEEN

Though it was a blood-streaked face and clothes-ripped Zeke who burst out of the bush and came loping up to him, Indian style, Marshal Houseman could see the stern determined lines on his deputy's face. The shooting he had just come through hadn't cowered him any. The boy had true grit.

'Why, you've been winged!' he said with some alarm, when he saw the damp dark stain on Zeke's right sleeve. Houseman reckoned that he would be white haired with fretting over his deputy's well-being before they made it back to Fort Smith.

'I'm OK, Marshal,' replied Zeke. 'It's only a graze. It's almost stopped bleeding. I've some cloths in my saddle-bag that will do as a bandage once I get my horse back.'

'How did you get into the shootin' scrape?' Houseman asked.

Zeke grinned. 'I kinda accidentally stumbled into one of the 'breeds coming out of the barn.' He then told Houseman how he had gunned him down and of being under fire from one of the dead man's *compadres*.

'So I figured it was wise to take to my heels,' Zeke continued. 'Hoping if I made it to Main Street the 'breed wouldn't risk shooting at me close to the sheriff's office. I was haring along this alley; I didn't know it ran alongside the whorehouse till this girl came out of a side door and dragged me inside.'

Houseman's eyebrows shot up. 'A cat-house girl?'

Zeke blushed. 'It isn't what you think, Marshal, she wasn't seeking business. She had seen Stacey and some of his gang pass by the mouth of the alley and being that she knew I was being hunted by one of Stacey's man she grabbed me to save me from running into a gunfight with the odds dead against me. I reckon she saved my life,' Zeke added soberly.

'There's a mite of charity in most sinners,' Houseman said, tongue-in-cheek.

'I'm finding that's true, Marshal,' replied Zeke. 'Bear Paw, a heathen Indian, and a girl who sells her body to lustful men, have both saved my life.'

'Yeah, well, now the ruckus is over and you're OK,' Houseman said brusquely, 'it's time we made our move. I've a feelin' that Stacey is about to burn down another farm soon. That fella Bear Paw cold-cocked was makin' his way along the street and he don't look a *hombre* who does much strollin' around so he could be goin' to pick up his horse and ride out of town. I'd like to know where and why. M'be we'll find out when we have our chat with that shyster when we ask him about Stacey's plans. Like when he's goin' to raid the next farm and hope it gives us time to send that wire to Fort Smith.' Houseman grinned savagely. 'We've got to throw one helluva scare into him so that he'll be forthcomin' in answerin' our questions.'

Zeke watched the marshal's face twist as though in pain as he thought of a way that would have the agent open up his sinful heart to them. To his surprise Houseman reached into his saddle-bag and drew out a big-bladed knife and handed it to him.

'Stick that down your belt, Deputy,' he said. 'And when we're talkin' to that agent fella act as though you're itchin' to use it, OK? And it would help if you had a kinda crazy look about you.'

Zeke slipped the knife into his belt thinking of how he could look crazy. He had a real puzzled look wondering what scheme the marshal had come up with to force the agent to talk.

FIFTEEN

Frazer wondered who it could be who was knocking at his door this late in the day. The elderly couple he had just seen were his last listed clients. He wasn't seeking any more penny-ante business from the town's citizens. The retainer he was receiving from Calvin T. Stricker was helping him to build up his capital so he could quit this dog dirt territory and its half-savage inhabitants and have a fancy office in Chicago and rub shoulders with big corporate lawyers. His snake oil salesman's smile barely concealed his annoyance at having the rest of his day disturbed.

His sour-gutted feeling came to the fore when he saw the two men standing on his stoop. The younger of the pair, a mere youth, face all scratched, was garbed as though he had taken time off from scaring away the crows from some cornfield. The elderly man, small thickset, grey stubbled, was dressed no grander. The pair of them had the cut of two saddle tramps seeking a handout. Until he noticed the stone-eyed look the old man was giving him. It made Stacey's mean-eyed glares positively friendly.

A nerve jumped painfully in his right cheek and choked off his angry, 'What the hell do you two bums want?' Switching his skin-deep smile back on he said, 'What can I do for you, gentlemen?'

His smile froze into a rictus-like grimace as the old man jammed a pistol into his belly, forcing him back into his office. Houseman back-heeled the door shut with such force that it rattled the building, and shook Frazer somewhat. He knew that the Strip swarmed with men who would have no compunction in robbing even their close kin, kill them if it came to the push. He began to panic.

'If, if it's money you want!' he blurted out. 'There's four hundred dollars in the safe! The keys are on the desk!'

Houseman took a step back from Frazer. 'Me and the boy ain't after your money,' he said with a look of fake indignation on his face. 'We ain't a coupla thievin' drifters. We've come here for a consultation.'

'A what!' gasped a surprised Frazer.

'Well not exactly a full blown, cash on the barrel-head kinda consultation,' Houseman told him. 'More like answerin' some pressin' questions me and the boy are fretting over.'

Frazer could see a glimmer of hope that he could get out of this dangerous situation without coming to any harm. It would mean humouring the crazy old bastard though. He forced a solemn look of concern on his face behare saying, 'Tell me about your problem, Mr—' He made a show of pulling out his watch from his vest pocket and checked the time. He gave a shadowy apologetic smile. 'But you'll have to be quick,

I've another appointment in about a half an hour.'

'We'll not take up much of your time,' Houseman replied giving him a toothy smile, a facial expression that caused Frazer's ray of hope to flicker. 'You just explain to us what your business with Mr Stacey is. The same Mr Stacey who bosses over a bunch of night riders who are burning out Injun farmers here in the Strip.'

'That's ridiculous!' Frazer said, shakey-voiced but trying to bluff it out. 'I don't do any business with a Mr Stacey!'

'Don't give us any forked-tongued shyster talk!' Houseman grated, eyes glinting angrily. 'We've seen you meetin' up with Stacey at that broken-down buildin' outside of town. We know Stacey has been busy raisin' up a gang. What for? Cattle liftin'? Bank-heistin'?' He gave a snort of a laugh. 'There ain't any cattle spreads or banks in the territory worth robbin'. The only big lawlessness goin' on in the Strip is the farm-raidin'. So puttin' two and two together we reckon that it's Stacey's wild bunch who are doin' the torchin'! And it so happens that you've been offerin' to buy the farms off the Injuns who have been raided. M'be you were just takin' advantage of some poor sodbusters' ill luck. I don't think so. I think that you're in cahoots with Stacey. You're the man who's payin' those raider's wages. Or frontin' for the fella who does.'

The sickness of fear swept up from Frazer's stomach gagging acidly at his throat. How much did the old bastard know about his dealings with Stacey? Enough to see him jailed'? He rested a hand on the desk behind him to keep him on his feet.

Houseman could see that his accusations had struck home. Frazer had the pinched-face look of a man about to lose control of his bladder. It was time to increase the pressure, with the help of his deputy plus a few lies. He fixed an evil-eyed stare on Frazer for a minute or two before speaking again.

A slack-jawed Frazer eyeballed Houseman back with the unblinking glazed-eyed look of a rabbit hypnotized by a sidewinder.

'A few weeks ago,' Houseman began, 'a white sodbuster's place was raided and his hired hand was gunned down. He happened to be my brother and this boy's pa. Now bein' that we're mountain folk it's only natural for the boy to be seekin' blood for blood. Ain't that so, Zeke?'

Zeke knew it was time for him to do his acting stint. Glaring-eyed he drew back his lips in a wolf-like snarl. To raise a few extra chills in the lawyer he pulled out the knife from under his coat, far enough for several inches of the razor-shape blade to be visible.

Frazer switched his gaze on to Zeke, and wished he hadn't. The hillbilly crow scarer had changed. He now had the merciless look of a savage Indian. The fearful knife he was fingering was making his bowels as loose as his bladder felt. And he was sure that the dark patch on his right coat sleeve he had never noticed on his first look at the boy, seemed like dried blood. The crazy kid's last victim's blood. Frazer cursed himself for thinking that even easy money didn't come without a price.

'Now put that hog sticker away, Zeke,' Houseman chided. 'Don't let it be said that we backwoods folk lack

manners. Give the gent time to answer our questions.'
He scowled at Frazer. 'But if he ain't forthcomin', well,
then you can give him a taste of our rough country
ways.'

Houseman weighed up the ashen-faced Frazer and
judged that the agent had swallowed their play acting
and was about to crack. 'I'd advise you to talk to us,
mister,' he said. 'It'll save you a whole heap of grief.
Zeke, ever since he could walk, has been cursed with
this crazy murderous streak. Why, even though I'm his
close kin when he's in one of his black moods I keep
well clear of him. He's likely to slash out with that big
bowie of his at the slightest upset. Since he heard of his
pa bein' killed I've been walkin' on eggs when I'm
around him.'

Frazer risked another quick glance at the 'upset' boy
and the knife he was still handling. He shuddered and
broke.

'I'll tell you all I know about Stacey and his raiding!'
the words blurting out. Then, regaining a little of his
lost courage, he said, 'How do I stand, will you go to
the sheriff and tell him I'm implicated in the fire-rais-
ing?' Frazer licked his lips nervously as he waited for
the decision from the fearsome-looking mountain
men. One that could see him locked in the state pen
for the next twenty years.

Houseman shook his head. He had to give a little,
the agent had said he was willing to talk. Stacey and his
hired guns were the men he wanted hauled back to
Fort Smith, or dead.

'No, this is personal business between me and the
boy and Stacey and his raidin' bastards,' he lied. He

nodded to the still scowling Zeke. 'I think I can persuade the boy here to forget about your role in the dirty business that killed his pa. But it would be advisable for you to quit doin' business hereabouts pronto like. If Stacey gets to hear that you've ratted on him before I rope him in then he'll seek you out and kill you, so start talkin' and m'be you'll be in time to catch the next stage outa town.'

Frazer talked. And Houseman found out the name of the man who had been paying Stacey and his gang's wages. 'My role was only a minor one, just going out and buying up the properties, that's all,' he finished, not daring to meet Houseman's beady-eyed gaze, or the boy's mad-eyed glare.

Houseman grunted. The statement the agent had just made was legal binding enough for him to accuse Stacey of murder and arson. It would be strong enough for Judge Parker to hang Stacey.

'One thing more before we leave you to pack,' Houseman said. 'I take it that you haven't handed the deeds of those farms you bought to Striker yet.'

Frazer nodded dumbly with the pained thousand-yard stare of a man who had seen his future rich-living world vanish in a matter of minutes.

'Good,' Houseman grinned. 'I'll take 'em.'

Frazer was past debating clients' rights and legal protocols; he had a greater urgency to put as much space between him and Stacey, and Striker as fast as he could. Maybe as far away as California where he could set up a new practice. Well clear of any farm burners. Bowed-shouldered he walked across to his safe.

*

'You oughta take up actin' instead of keepin' the peace, Deputy,' Houseman said. He grinned. 'You put a scare in me back there fingerin' that knife with a face as homely lookin' as an Apache bronco, let alone frighten Frazer into pourin' his heart out.'

They were back among the trees where Houseman had tied up his horse, the marshal turning over in his mind the information Frazer had given about the raiders and how to use it to their advantage. Striker, the money man in Chicago, he would leave to the judge to deal with. He thin-grinned. 'Now we know we're up against two gangs of fire-raisers. It's about time we held a council of war, so to speak, to find the best way we can put paid to the sonsuvbitches.'

'Can't we just go to the sheriff and tell him that Stacey and his 'breeds are the raiders, Marshal?' Zeke asked. 'After all, he's the law in Bitter Water Springs.'

'We could,' replied Houseman. 'But if the sheriff arrests Stacey and his gang Stacey will drag Frazer down with him. Name him as the man who hired them and I promised the agent I'd try and keep him in the clear. And there's another reason why I ain't goin' to the sheriff, Deputy. You well know that they ain't *hombres* who'd raise their arms meekly when asked to by the sheriff. There'd be one helluva gunfight, in the saloon, or out in the street, and innocent bystanders could be harmed.' Houseman did some more face twisting, concentrating before he spoke again.

'We could find out which trail that raider took when he rode out. I strongly figure he's left town. If I'm right then he's ridin' out to meet up with the extra men Frazer told us Stacey had hired.' Houseman grinned.

140

'It should be a piece of cake for an old tracker like yours truly, to find the spot where four, five men have made camp and read their sign.'

Noticing his deputy's doubtful look, Houseman said, 'It won't be so hard as it seems findin' the camp. They'll have been bedded down not far outa town, close by sweet runnin' water. Once we've found out just how many of the sonsuvbitches there are I'll send that wire to the judge tellin' him to get that band of marshals he promised me high-tailin' it out here, pronto. We'll try and keep an eye on the raiders till the marshals show up,' he added lamely.

Zeke didn't rate Marshal Houseman's plan very highly. How could they keep an eye on two gangs of raiders? Come dark they could ride out to burn some farm so which bunch would they track? What farm they could be raiding chewed away at Zeke's guts.

He was having deep, uneasy thoughts about the dangerous situation facing the Paxton family, the sweet smiling Sarah Jane in particular, if the marshal's dire warning that the raiders could attack the farm again, was proved right. They ought to be with the Paxtons giving them extra protection, instead of going off on a hare-brained chase trying to trail a bunch of raiders who could already be on their way to destroy some farmer's life's work. Zeke's blood chilled. Maybe Mr Paxton's. He didn't think he had the authority to question Marshal Houseman's actions being that he was only a newly sworn in deputy. He was duty bound to carry out the marshal's say so.

'You go back to the barn the same way as you came here, Deputy,' Houseman said. 'But keep outa sight when you get there, then you won't stir up any more trouble. I'll pick up your horse and ask the smith about Stacey's pard, OK?'

Zeke nodded his OK then handed the marshal his knife back. He didn't want to stab himself with it when scrambling through the brush. And he sure wasn't willing enough to use it to defend himself if he ran into the 'breeds again. Houseman watched him disappear into the undergrowth and untie his horse and swing into the saddle. Pulling his hat low down over his face he kneed his mount into a walk, out into the open.

He also was having worrying thoughts about the Paxtons being on their own, but he thought that trying to break up the gang before they raided the farm seemed to be the best move in a bad situation. Finding out that there were now two gangs didn't make his task look good at all. Things could go badly wrong for him and the boy and the judge could be reading a wire back there in his chanbers notifying him of the gunning down of two of his marshals. Houseman didn't stop cursing until he drew up his horse outside the livery barn.

SIXTEEN

They were about two miles out of Bitter Water Springs when Houseman gave the order to pull up their mounts.

'That crick the smith told me about, Deputy,' Houseman said, 'where he saw a four-man camp when he passed by this way with his wagon the other day, can't be that far ahead so we'd better be prepared for trouble.'

Houseman had picked up Zeke's horse, its shoe repaired by the smith for free, the smith saying that a man who sent one of Stacey's bully boys to hell where he belonged was entitled to a favour.

'That 'breed almost put paid to me with his wild shootin',' the smith said.

Houseman grinned. 'Two bully boys sent wingin' their way to hell, friend. The boy downed one in the saloon a coupla days ago.'

'Well I'll be damned!' gasped the smith. 'He's the kid who out-shot Clegg? The young *pistolero* deserves a free new saddle. Is he OK? Another one of Stacey's

143

'breeds was cuttin' loose at him across there at the back lots.'

'He's OK,' repeated Houseman. 'But I told him to lie low until I got hold of his horse.' He paused for a moment before speaking again. The smith by his talk bore no friendship for Stacey so there would be no chance of him warning the gang leader that someone was asking nosy questions about him.

'Like you, friend,' he said, 'Me and the boy ain't pals of Stacey. Right now we're tryin' to track down one of Stacey's boys, a fella sportin' a bandage round his head bein' one of my boys cracked it open with his pistol. He was headin' towards here and I think he's rode out of town to meet up with a bunch of hard men someplace near. You could m'be put me right.'

The smith gave Houseman a long quizzical look. 'You don't look like a lawman to me,' he said. 'So you ain't bein' paid to track down Logan, that's the name of the fella you saw, so it must be personal, but that's none of my business except to tell you that don't bite off more than you can chaw just to settle some griev-ance with Stacey. He bosses over a real mean bunch. As you figured, mister, Logan rode outa town by the east trail. M'be to meet up with the four men camped along Beaver crick, three miles or so along the trail. I saw them there the other day when I was bringin' a plough in on my wagon to repair.'

Houseman thanked the smith for his information and the shoeing of Zeke's horse, then taking hold of the reins of both horses made his way to the rear of the barn and the waiting Zeke, leaving the smith scratch-ing his head thinking that hurt pride, or whatever, was going to put the old man and the boy into early graves on Boot Hill.

Zeke watched the marshal pull out another pistol from his saddle-bag, check the loads before stuffing it in the waistband of his pants Then he drew out his holstered pistol, checked its action and slipped it back into its holster.

Zeke thought that he'd better check his own pistol, but curious to know what his partner's wild plan was he said, 'You mentioned trouble, Marshal, what trouble would that be?'

'If Logan is at the crick with those fellas we'll know for sure that they're part of Stacey's gang,' Houseman said. 'Logan was the fella who had his knife in your back. As you well know we've no legal authority here in the Strip but we're bone-fide US marshals and if fired on by some lawbreakers we are, as marshals, entitled to defend ourselves by arrestin' or gunnin' down the shootists.'

'Are those fellas at the crick going to shoot at us, Marshal?' a still confused Zeke asked.

Houseman gave a fierce twist of a grin. 'When we start that trouble I mentioned, like fire-ballin' in on their camp, I reckon they'll fire back at us.'

'They will that, Marshal,' was all that Zeke could come out with. He didn't ask the marshal why he had abandoned his first plan, that of sending a wire to Fort Smith for the extra marshals while they kept watch on the fire-raisers. He guessed that the old man had realized that they couldn't keep two gangs under constant observation. It was the best choice he could make taking on the gang themselves. Even though, Zeke thought, it could get them both dead, leaving the Paxton farm wide open to the raiders. Zeke didn't dwell on that bitter thought long. He gave a deep sigh, it was trusting in God's goodness time again.

As if reading his thoughts Houseman said, 'I know that it's a different plan to what we intended carryin' out, Deputy, but conditions have changed. Ahead of us, if they're still there, are half of Stacey's gang, five men. If we go in on dust-raisin' horses shootin' and a-hollerin', we can put paid to the sonsuvbitches, or scatter them.' He gave another of his savage grins. 'That's if you can fire as true up on a fast-movin' horse as you can standing on your feet.'

Zeke didn't try to imagine what it would be like riding maybe a hundred or so yards under fire from five out and out sinners. The marshal seemed to think that the odds were in their favour. Zeke licked at dried lips. He would soon find out if the old marshal's reasoning was right. All he knew was that he was being called upon to cause the shedding of more blood than he thought he would have to do when proudly pinning on his marshal's badge at Fort Smith. He pulled out his pistol, emptied out the six loads and thumbed fresh shells into the chambers and slipped it back into its sheath. Zeke was a firm believer in God aiding those who helped themselves.

It was Lonny. a small weasel-faced man, who saw Houseman and Zeke first. 'Two riders standin' eyein' the camp, boys!' he called out. His three *compadres* stopped the saddling of their mounts and looked across the creek. 'They look like a coupla drifters to me hopin' to get a handout from us,' continued Lonny.

'Well, they'll be unlucky then,' Logan said, as he threw his coffee dregs on the fire then toed dirt on to the dying embers. 'Because it's time for you fellas to earn your pay.'

'Logan's there, so they're a bunch of owlhoots all right.' Houseman said. 'That means any law-abidin' citizen, let alone US marshals, can shoot them on sight. OK let's go and do it.' He dug his heels into his horse's flanks; the startled animal took off in a high leg-kicking dust-raised gallop. He had covered five yards of ground before Zeke had jabbed his mount forward into a run.

'Why, the bastards are comin' in on us!' yelled Lonny and yanked his rifle out of its boot, levered a shell into the chamber and brought it up to his shoulder. The spray kicked up by the two horses as they came across the creek prevented him from getting a clear sighting of either rider. Shooting down the horses was like throwing away good money. They could be sold for hard cash once the sons-of-bitches up on their backs had been blown out of their saddles. And he was out of their pistol range, or so he thought, until they had cleared the creek. He raised his pressure on the trigger and waited – a brief but fatal delay that cost him his life.

Through the watery haze Houseman caught a fleeting glimpse of a rifle-holding man and the long-barrelled Walker Colt he held in his left hand boomed and flamed. To Zeke, riding close behind him, it sounded like the discharge of a small field piece. Lonny was flung back against his horse as the heavy calibre shell punched a hole in his forehead, shattering the back of his skull into a bloody mush as it exited.

As his mount pounded up the slight rise from the creek Houseman began firing with both of his pistols as fast as he could draw back the hammers, clinging to his saddle by the seat of his pants and hard dug in knees. Zeke was saving his six loads until he got nearer to the camp, wanting every shot to pay.

Houseman's deadly hail cut down another of the hired guns; the remaining two decided that they hadn't been paid to have a standup gunfight with two mad-assed *pistoleros* turned and made a run for it. Zeke, firing single spaced shots, had them both tumbling face down into the dust. With his blood racing wild he surprised himself by howling like a bronco Indian touching coup. He saw Logan getting into his saddle from the blind side of his horse and triggered off his last load and Logan slid back out of his sight. Then he was pulling up his horse in a haunch sliding, spark-raising halt on top of the smoking ashes of the fire. He quickly rammed two shells into his pistol and recocked it. Warily he edged his horse foward until he could see Logan lying spreadeagled and unmoving on the ground.

'We've downed all of them, Marshal!' he called out, the pistol wavering in a sweat-glazed hand. He felt as drained of strength as though he had run all the way from the farside of the creek. He looked round and saw Houseman slumped in his saddle, face creased with pain. Alarmed he pushed the pistol into the waist-band of his pants and jumped down from his horse and ran over to the marshal.

Before he could ask him how badly he was hurt

Houseman growled, 'Help me down, Deputy.' He reached down and rested a steadying hand on Zeke's shoulder and with much groaning and cursing he eased himself to the ground to stand there shaking-legged. Beneath the open jacket Zeke saw the growing dark stain on the marshal's shirt just above his left hip. Houseman pointed with his chin at the two gunmen Zeke had shot down. 'One of those bastards put a slug through me,' he snarled.

'You're bleeding badly,' Zeke said. 'I'll get some cloths out of my saddle-bag and try and bandage up the wound.'

'You just get the cloths, Deputy, I'll dress it,' Houseman snapped. 'It's a clean through shot, painful, but it ain't a bad wound.' He hard-eyed Zeke. 'You've got more important business to see to than bandaging an old fart's scratches. You've to ride back to the Paxtons, pronto like.'

Zeke nodded over his shoulder at the dead men. 'Aren't we going to see them decently buried, Marshal? They're beyond any sinning now.'

'You've got to make a choice, Deputy,' Houseman said flat-voiced. 'Either stay here and plant those no-good outlaws, or have to help bury the fine Paxton family.'

Zeke's face drained of blood, the fever of the few savage minutes of the gunfight now an icy chill in his bones. He frantically wondered about how he could have forgotten about the danger the Paxtons could be facing from Stacey and the vicious 'breeds.

'Will you be OK, Marshal, being wounded an' all?' he asked.

'Yeah, yeah, I can tend to myself,' Houseman replied irritably. 'You go and get those cloths and you can be on your way.' He wanted to be on his own so that he could curse himself to his heart's content at allowing some penny-ante road agent shoot him. And to get a few pulls at the whiskey bottle just to help to ease the pain somewhat.

Zeke was mounted up ready to ride out. He cast an anxious gaze at the marshal dabbing gingerly at his wound, low cursing as he did so. Straight-faced he said, 'Pa once told me that the devil's drink had one good use, if poured on a wound it would prevent it from going bad. I figure you oughta have enough left in that bottle you have in your saddle-bag, Marshal, to do that and have some over to have your regular nightly drink as well.' He pulled his mount's head round and in a flurry of dust rode out of the camp of dead men.

A slack-jawed surprised Houseman watched him go. For a moment he forget his pain as he wondered which of the two of them was the hayseed. It looked as though he was. Deputy Marshal Ezekiel Isaiah Butler hadn't missed a trick. . . .

SEVENTEEN

There was still a couple of hours of daylight left when Stacey and the 'breeds dismounted well away from the farm. This was a vengeance raid, a killing raid, so they were going to close in on the farm on foot to make sure their firing was quick and accurate.

'There'll be a lookout up on that ridge ahead of us, boys,' Stacey said. 'So we'll sneak up on that sodbuster from the west with the sun at our backs.' He grinned wolfishly. 'They won't know we're among them until they hear the shot that kills them.'

Paxton, Bear Paw and his uncle were on the ridge, Paxton openly showing himself. The farm had to appear normal, Ma and Sarah Jane feeding the stock, Dave, later on, coming up on the ridge to relieve him. The raiders would expect a place that they had tried to burn down before would have posted a lookout. Bear Paw and Dark Cloud were lying low only a few feet from the farmer. Bear Paw's two cousins were some-where on the farside of the house and, although Paxton glanced regularly in that direction he could see no sign of them. Though he had to admit the farm was well protected, having to face another night of fearful expectations worried him sick. He almost wished that the raiders would come and get things settled, one way or another.

Paxton heard the sudden trilling but clear carrying sound of some bird behind him, then further round its mate answering it. He didn't think anything of it until he noticed that Bear Paw and his uncle had grabbed hold of their rifles and exchanged significant glances.

Bear Paw looked up at Paxton. 'There're here, four of them!'

'Where? How do you know?' Paxton scrabbled to his feet, face showing his alarm.

Bear Paw reached up a hand and dragged him down. 'Just act naturally, Mr Paxton. Go down to the house and get your family indoors, nice and slowly. My cousins will see that they will come to no harm.'

'How do you know the sonsuvbitches are here, Bear Paw?' Paxton asked.

Bear Paw grinned. 'Those birds you heard were Billy and George, my cousins.'

'Well I'll be durned!' Paxton gasped. Somehow he kept control of emotions and stood up and stretched himself as a man would do after squatting down for a length of time. Just before he set off down the slope he saw that he had only been speaking to Bear Paw. Dark Cloud had silently vanished.

Bear Paw answered his unasked question. 'He's gone to join in the killing,'

'Ain't we goin' to help them?' Paxton said. 'It's my place they've come to burn.'

Bear Paw shook his head. 'It's an honour killing. Dark Cloud and his sons' business. They'd be insulted if we joined in.' He smiled. 'And they need no help.'

Paxton descended the slope with a more settled mind than he'd had since the night of the first raid.

Orozco stopped his gliding through the trees for a moment or two when he heard the bird sounds. Somewhere in the dark recesses of his mind his father's Indian blood sounded a faint warning bell. He took a quick but all-seeing glance about him but couldn't see or hear anything that should alarm him. He looked across at Silvero and Leon and saw them moving forward without any holding back. Further to his right Stacey punched at the air with his fist; a signal that they had to cross the open ground to the shack at a run. Orozco lengthened his stride and got himself killed a split second faster that Billy Grey Wolf had planned.

Orozco stopped in his tracks as though he had hit an invisible wall as a bare to the waist Indian boy, shedding leaves and dirt, sprang up out of the ground in front of him. Cursing he frantically tried to bring his rifle round. Billy Grey Wolf fired his Winchester from the hip. Orozco felt a hammer blow on his chest, a few seconds of fearful pain as the blood poured thick and dark from his mouth. Just before everything went black for him his dying brain registered another shot, the shot from Billy's brother's gun that killed Leon.

Silvero heard the two shots and could no longer see his two *compadres* moving through the timber. Stacey, who should be on his right, was also gone. He was on his own.

Stacey, as soon as he heard the shots feared, the worst: he was heading into an ambush. The sodbuster had killed six of his boys, the son-of-a-bitch wasn't about to put paid to him. He turned and ran fast to where they had left the horses, cold sweating with fear, expecting at any moment the killing back shot.

Silvero, for the first time in his life, began to panic. That unusual feeling didn't last long. He heard a slight rustling sound behind him but before he could swing round strong hands grabbed his shoulders. He felt the icy sharpness of a knife slicing across his throat followed by the warm stickiness of blood pouring down his chest. A stone-faced Dark Cloud pushed the sagging-legged fast-dying Silvero away from him as he folded up all the way to the ground. 'The white-eye has escaped!' He called over to his sons. 'Get him before he reaches his horse!' The brothers sped back through the trees in a hunting loop. After a satisfied look at the man he had killed Dark Cloud cupped his hand to his mouth and gave out a killing whoop to alert Bear Paw that the danger to the farm was over.

The pale-faced Paxtons, clutching their mixture of firearms, heard the whoop and prayed that it was good tidings. It was not until Bear Paw shouted into the cabin that the raiders had been killed did they know that their prayers had been answered. They broke into tears and smiles and rushed out of the cabin to hug Bear Paw.

Zeke had forced his mount at a cruel panting, foam-flecked-mouthed pace upwards as he neared the ridge overlooking the farm, fearful that he would smell the smoke of burning barns or see the flames of a burning home reaching into the darkening sky. In a hollow to his left he saw four horses. He was too late; the raiders were already attacking the farm. And against all his strict religious upbringing he came out with one of Marshal Houseman's curse words. He dug his heels into his mount to urge it on for that last mile to the farm vowing that he would kill Stacey and the 'breeds even if it meant sacrificing his own life.

At a bend in the trail he almost ran down Stacey. Zeke dragged his horse to a halt and reached wildly under his coat for his pistol, knowing with cold fear that he would be too late to help the Paxtons. Stacey had his rifle trained on him.

A rifle shot rang out and Stacey seemed to have difficulty in holding up his rifle. There came another shot and Stacey dropped heavily to the ground, thick dust rising around him. Zeke suddenly faced two bare-chested Indians, boys about his age.

'I'm Deputy Butler,' he said. 'That fella you've shot, just before he shot me, is the boss of a gang of raiders! Are the Paxtons OK?' His words came out wild and fast.

The two brothers grinned at each other. 'They're OK,' Billy said. 'We've just killed the last of them.'

Zeke flopped back in his saddle, trying hard not to cry in front of the Indian boys. Sarah Jane was safe! 'Thanks for saving my life. Stacey had the drop on me.' He smiled. 'Who am I thanking and how come you're here at the Paxtons?'

It was George who answered him. 'Bear Paw is our cousin; he asked our pa for help to save the Paxton farm from the raiders who burnt down our farm.'

'Well I'll be damned and blasted!' Zeke blurted out, back sliding again into Marshal Houseman's coarse language. Bear Paw had well and truly redeemed himself. He watched the brothers cross the trail to gather up the dead raiders' horses before he headed for the farm, a much-more-at-ease-with-himself Zeke, though tempered with the nagging worry of how the marshal was making out on the trail.

Zeke could only see Bear Paw when he dismounted outside the house and when he came up to him he told Bear Paw that he had met his cousins.

'And I wouldn't be talking to you if I hadn't,' he said soberly. 'They shot Stacey just as he was about to put paid to me. They told me about you asking for their help. Me and the marshal and the Paxtons will always be beholden to you, Bear Paw.'

'I was only doing my duty as a marshal, Zeke,' Bear Paw said. 'Keeping the peace.' He smiled. 'Marshal Houseman forgot to unswear me as a deputy before I rode out.' His face hardened. 'Where is Marshal Houseman? And you look as though you've got a wounded arm! What happened back there in Bitter Water Springs?'

Zeke told him of the gunfight with the other band of raiders and how the marshal had been wounded.

'He's OK,' he said. 'Just that it's painful for him to ride. And with his so-called gut-feeling about the raiders hitting the Paxton soon, he ordered me to get here with all speed to back them up.' He grinned. 'I've raised the sweat on my horse for nothing.' Somewhat disappointed at not seeing Sarah Jane, he asked Bear Paw where everyone was.

'Mr Paxton and his son are burying the dead raiders; Dark Cloud is checking that his boys have shot the last of them.' Bear Paw half-turned, then grinned. 'And here's the girl you've been casting your eyes about for.'

Zeke also swung round to see Sarah Jane, skirt scuffing the dust, running towards him.

Not feeling any embarrassment at Bear Paw standing there, Sarah Jane flung her arms round Zeke. 'The raiders have all been killed!' she sobbed. 'The farm's saved!'

A moon-faced smiling Zeke felt her tear-damp cheek on his as he held her tight.

Sarah Jane suddenly stepped back a pace from him. Horrified she touched his left arm. 'You're wounded!' she cried. looked wildly about her. 'Where's Marshal Houseman?'

'He's OK, Sarah Jane,' replied Zeke. 'Like me he's been wounded but he oughta be riding in soon.'

'Come inside,' Sarah Jane said. 'And I'll clean up your wound.'

'I have to water my horse first,' Zeke said. 'Then ride along the trail a piece to wait for the marshal. Then I'll—'

'I'll see to your horse, Deputy, and ride out to meet the marshal,' Bear Paw said.

Zeke shot him a grateful glance and Sarah Jane took hold of his hand and led him into the house, Zeke thinking that it had been worth getting shot.

What fearful sight he could be riding into, a burnt-out farm, his deputy and the Paxtons lying wounded or dead and the slow pace he was making, had Houseman

157

running out of fresh curse words. What he hadn't expected to see was Bear Paw riding up to him. 'Why, what are you doin' here?' he asked with some alarm in his voice. 'Has there been trouble at the Paxtons? Did Deputy Butler make it here OK?'

Bear Paw smiled. 'He's OK. So is everyone on the farm. The raiders paid a call but my uncle and his two boys killed them all.' Houseman listened with ever widening eyes as Bear Paw told him of all that had happened since he had said his farewells to him and Zeke.

Houseman gave him a long look before he spoke. 'I intended to leave you to take your chances at White Oaks, but my deputy prevailed on me to take you with us. And I tell you this, Bear Paw, if I live to be a hundred, I'll never make a better decision, and that's the goddamned truth. Now let's get to the Paxtons,' he growled. 'Before I run outa blood; I'm bleedin' like an arrow-shot hog.'

The Paxton family were getting back to doing their normal everyday chores, Paxton and Dave chopping kindling, Mrs Paxton busy in the kitchen and Sarah Jane feeding the chickens with Zeke following her about like a devoted hound dog. Bear Paw and his kin, with much hand shaking and hugs, had ridden out, a pleased Dark Cloud with the deeds of the Indian farms in his pocket. Houseman, having had his wound seen to by Mr Paxton, not wanting Mrs Paxton to see his holey and dirty woollen undershirt, was sitting on the porch stoop thinking of his deputy's future – if Zeke was going to have much of a future being his pard.

Paxton, seeing the marshal's dour look, put down his axe and walked over to him and asked him if his wound was playing him up.

'Nah,' replied Houseman. 'I'm just worried about my deputy. He's been in more shootin' scrapes in the short time he's rode with me than I've taken part in a whole year of marshallin'.'

'But he's pulled through them OK, Marshal,' Paxton replied.

'Yeah, that's so,' Houseman said. 'But how long do you reckon that good fortune's goin' to last, eh? He's too good a boy to fall foul of some no-good bush-whacker's gun.'

'Him gettin' shot would upset Sarah Jane no end,' Paxton said softly. 'She's grown mighty fond of him.'

Houseman thought for a moment before saying, 'I've got to go to Bitter Water Springs to wire the judge that the trouble out here is over. While I'm there I'll try my damnedest to persuade old Blakemore to take the boy on as one of his deputies. He owes me a big favour for taking care of those raiders for him. Keepin' the peace there ain't as shootin' risky as huntin' down bad-asses in the Territory. That's if I can get the kid to take the job. He's got this foolish hankerin' of wantin' to be a marshal.'

Paxton grinned. 'If you tell him that Sarah Jane makes regular trips there with the supply wagon that could m'be swing him round to your way of thinkin'.'

Houseman's face brightened up. 'That could work.' He grinned. 'Then I could get myself a whiskey-drinkin' pard. It's been hell tryin' to sneak a pull at the bottle when I thought the kid wasn't lookin'. It was

159

gettin' to be as though I'd signed the pledge.'

His grin broadened. 'When Zeke plucks up enough courage to ask your girl to marry him, you tell him that me and Bear Paw will expect to be invited to the wedding.'